Liszt

CLAUDE ROSTAND

Translated by John Victor

Illustrated Calderbook CB 78

CALDER AND BOYARS – LONDON

First published in Great Britain in 1972
by Calder & Boyars Ltd
18 Brewer Street, London W1

Originally published in French in 1960
by Editions du Seuil Paris

© Editions du Seuil, 1960
© This translation Calder & Boyars Ltd 1972

ISBN 0 7145 0342 8 Cloth edition
ISBN 0 7145 0343 6 Paper edition

Typeset by
Specialised Offset Services Ltd., Liverpool
and Printed by
T. & A. Constable Ltd., Hopetoun Street, Edinburgh

Liszt

CLAUDE ROSTAND

Contents

Appendices

Assemblage étonnant   de génie et d'enfance

Il a dévancé   l'avenir;

Et dans l'âge   de l'espérance

Fait déjà naître   un souvenir.

Par un amateur

FRANÇOIS LISZT,

âge de 11 ans

à Paris, chez Martinet

You belong to art, not to the Church,
but women make me frightened for you.
Adam Liszt

PUTZI or 'LE PETIT LITZ'

It is the night of 21 to 22 October 1811, in a small, half-peasant, half-middle-class house surrounded by a garden full of autumn flowers. Occasional stable noises can be heard nearby and, in the distance, lost in the silence of the Hungarian plains, are a few tumbledown cottages. In this house a boy has just been born, the boy who is later on to hold such attraction for women conceived between two Napoleonic battles.

A frail creature who was to linger for several years on the verge of life and death, Franz Liszt was the son of Adam Liszt, accountant and estate manager of Prince Esterhazy, and of Anna Lager, an Austrian girl from Krems, a ravishing young brunette with large eyes and a sensual mouth, endowed with all the charm of the Viennese. Adam had married Anna the previous year, while he was still employed at the castle of Eisenstadt, where the pace of life was extremely fast.

Anna Liszt   *Adam Liszt*

Adam Liszt was passionately fond of music. He played the flute, violin and guitar and was an excellent pianist. While at the castle, he had known Haydn, Cherubini and Hummel. Esterhazy, intending to please him on the occasion of his marriage, had promoted him to the management of one of his estates, that of Raiding (a village of the district of Oedenburg, not far from the Austrian frontier and called in Hungarian Dobrjàn). But to the young couple this seemed rather like exile, despite the material advantages. During the day Adam would supervise the weighing of corn, and in the evenings he and his wife would make music together. In October 1811, during the late stages of her pregnancy, a comet was observed, and Anna watched it every evening. It was a good omen and, as luck would have it, it was still shining on the night of Franz's birth. The next day, gipsies came to play

8

outside the little wooden fence encircling the manager's garden, to celebrate the birth of the baby who was later to call himself 'gipsy and Franciscan'.

Next to boredom, anxiety was to be the dominant feature of the family's life at Raiding. For the first six years, young Franz was constantly ailing: fevers, fainting fits, nervous breakdowns followed one after the other. There was a day when he was thought to be dead, and the village carpenter even began to assemble the timber for a tiny coffin. The doctors had given up hope weeks ago. But nature worked its miracle and Franz began to play again, he suddenly developed physically, filled out in the face and, most interesting of all, acquired that penetrating, haughty, yet gentle expression which was to be with him all his life. Already, music was his first interest. He listened to the singing in church and followed gipsies round from door to door. The fascination they held for him was to be demonstrated later on in a book of which he seems, however, not to have been the sole author.

'Few things fired our imagination more in early youth than the glaring enigma of the Bohemians, begging a miserable coin before every palace and cottage in exchange for a few words murmured in the ear, a few dance tunes which no wandering fiddler could ever imitate, a few songs for setting lovers aflame but not invented by lovers. What questions we asked when we were very small in order to discover the explanation of this charm, to which everyone fell victim but which no-one could define! But it was no good; one *felt* this charm, but one could not explain it. Being but the weak apprentice of a stern master, we knew no other access to the world of fantasy than what we could perceive through the scaffolding of well organised sounds. This made us all the more curious to understand the fascination wrought by those calloused hands as they grated the bow over their inferior instruments or set the brass ringing with such imperious urgency. At the same time, we were haunted in our daydreams by those coppery faces that the sun itself could not darken further, prematurely ruined by the intemperate seasons and by the undisciplined, one might say galvanising, emotions of their disorderly life.'

From the outset, music and adventure were to mark Liszt's life. The 'stern master' could be his father. Not that his father pushed him towards music but, in his own enthusiasm for the piano, Adam did introduce him to a repertoire which, although somewhat limited in its appeal, nevertheless attracted Franz. One day he had been playing the Concerto in C sharp minor by Ries — which would seem to prove that he had a rather fine technique — and, that very evening, the child, now six years old, sang the first theme of it and reproduced it quite skilfully on the piano. From that moment all was decided, and Adam decreed that his son should be a pianist.

His progress was astonishing. In three years Franz had become sufficiently skilled to appear in public, and his first concert was in 1820. It was a charity concert for the benefit of a blind musician. Charity was also one of Liszt's vocations. So often did he play for the benefit of others that the only legacy he left was his soutane, four shirts and seven pocket handkerchieves. This first concert took place at Oedenburg. Franz amazed the public by his performance of the Concerto in E flat by Ries, and even more by the way he improvised on popular themes.

Other concerts were to follow immediately, notably at Eisenstadt, but above all at Pressburg, where a group of Hungarian nobles decided, after hearing him play, to offer the child a bursary which would allow him a more complete and serious pursuit of his studies. Adam asked for leave from the Prince and left with Franz for Weimar to seek lessons from Johann Nepomuk Hummel; but the price was rather high and father and son installed themselves at Vienna, where they remained during 1821 and 1822. There, Franz worked at the piano with Czerny who, filled with enthusiasm for his young pupil, refused to let him pay for his lessons, and he studied harmony and composition with Salieri, who had been one of the later teachers of Beethoven.

In December 1822, Liszt made his first appearance on a Viennese concert platform, to play the Concerto in E minor by Hummel. He also indulged in what was for a time to be one of his favourite acrobatic exercises, improvisation. On that particular day it was an astonishing piece of bravura using the theme of the Allegretto from the Seventh Symphony of Beethoven and an air from Rossini's *Zelmira*. This was a triumph, and on the next day a critic wrote: *'Est deus in nobis!'* Little Putzi, as Czerny had nicknamed him, had become the man of the moment.

1823   The Liszts stayed in Vienna until the end of the summer. It was during this period that the memorable encounter with Beethoven occurred. Things went badly at first. It was an obsession with Liszt to meet Beethoven. The latter, however, irritated by the success which was being accorded by the Viennese at the time to the most facile Italian music, was passing through a particularly difficult phase. Czerny, who was a friend of Schindler, managed, however, to arrange a meeting for Liszt, the details of which are not known, but it could not have been a very fortunate one since, if one is to believe the *Conversation Notebooks,* Schindler reproved Beethoven for his bad temper with Putzi. On 12 April he wrote to Beethoven: 'Don't you think you should repair the rather disagreeable reception you gave young Liszt recently by going to his concert tomorrow? It would be a great encouragement for the boy. Promise me you will go.' And in fact the young Liszt saw Beethoven once more on the 12th, and there is an entry in the notebook in his round hand: 'I have already expressed so often to Herr Schindler my desire to make your treasured acquaintance that I am happy this should now be possible. I am giving a concert on Sunday, 13th, and would respectfully beg that you grant me the honour of your presence.' Beethoven promised nothing but, according to one of the various versions left to us of the interview (by Schindler) he asked the child to play him something. Liszt played the Fugue in C minor from the *Well-tempered Klavier,* and when he had finished it, transposed it immediately with the utmost ease to a different key. 'What a cunning child,' cried Beethoven, 'the little scamp!' Finding himself thus encouraged, Liszt is then said to have played the first movement of the Concerto in C minor, which Beethoven received with the remark: 'Well now, you are one of the lucky ones, and you will make others happy, too! What could be more splendid than that!'

Next day, there was Beethoven, in the crowded Redoutensaal. The scene has been the subject of many an engraving and calendar. When Franz had played a Hummel concerto and a Fantasia of his own composition, Beethoven got up, mounted the platform and embraced the child amid prolonged applause.

Beethoven embraces Liszt
after his concert on 13 April, 1823

In the autumn the Liszts began a tour of concerts in Munich, Stuttgart and Strasbourg. All had triumphant receptions and finally, on 11 December, they arrived in Paris, where they installed themselves at the Hotel d'Angleterre, 11 rue du Mail, just opposite Erard's piano workshop. Their first call was to see Cherubini, the Director of the Conservatoire. Cherubini, cross-grained and pulling worried faces, greeted the young Hungarian with a categorical refusal on the grounds that the rules of the Conservatoire did not allow access to foreigners; strange quirk of French administration, particularly as expressed by Cherubini who, although Director of this same Conservatoire, had never been able to speak correct French!

But the Liszts' disappointment was short-lived. They had come to Paris with numerous letters of recommendation and all doors were to open without difficulty to the young prodigy. From the worldly point of view his two most useful protectors were Louis-Philippe (as he was to become) and Caroline, Duchesse de Berry. The former showered toys on him, including a 'pulcinella' which had amused 'le petit Litz' when he had been to play with the young Duc de Nemours. Caroline, whom the lithographer Delpech shows to have been in the bloom of an extraordinary beauty at twenty-five, opened her *salons* to him, and 'le petit Litz' won over the whole of society, probably more by his acrobatic qualities as a pianist than by his profound musical genius. The Franciscan-to-be launched himself on a gipsy string: he knew it all, retained it all, sensed it all. The 'clever monkey' commanded more attention than the inventive genius was to do later on.

But he did not let himself become too intoxicated. Although the piano-builder Sébastien Erard had adopted him, both out of affection and out of a perfectly legitimate taste for star publicity, 'le petit Litz' was also thinking of serious matters. There were composition lessons with Ferdinand Paër and counterpoint with Anton Reicha. It was Paër, too, who taught him the language he was to speak best and to prefer for the rest of his life: French. Liszt was always to speak incorrect German and to retain no more than a meagre acquaintance with his mother tongue.

1824   Winter came and went in a series of uninterrupted successes. But the real moment of public triumph came on 8 March. The Prince had offered 'le petit Litz' the Italian Opera. La Pasta, that singer for whom Stendhal had such high praise (not that that was an absolute recommendation) came to sing two arias at the young prodigy's first concert. This kind of collaboration was much practised in those freakish but charitable times. Some days later, the triumph was repeated at the *'Concert spirituel'*. Liszt was the darling of Paris. It was hard to imagine that this child, this musician of the extreme right, protégé of princes, was soon to become the friend of Lamennais, the disciple of Saint-Simon, thus becoming known as 'left-wing' at a time when it was less intellectually fashionable than now, and playing into the hands of his rival, Thalberg.

Paër, one time conductor of the Imperial orchestra, suggested to the Paris Opéra that the thirteen-year-old Liszt should be commissioned to

13

1824 (drawing by Leprince)

write a one-act opera: this was *Don Sanche ou le château d'amour*, the libretto of which had been entrusted by Paër to two mediocre hack-writers, Théaulon and Rancé. It was to be a 'light opera', so Franz's teacher said. The two versifiers immediately set to and the work was accepted even before it was finished.

During this time, Sébastien Érard was being very kind — very generous in fact – but not losing his head where piano sales were concerned. The phenomenal young Liszt seemed to him to be a very good connection. Moreover this was precisely the time when he was hoping to launch in Europe his newly perfected instrument, the double escapement piano. The English market looked favourable, and as soon as spring came he organised a tour for Liszt during the London season, George IV and the court being quite curious to make his acquaintance. The reception there was the same as in Paris. Liszt was accepted immediately. He played at Court and the nobility vied for him. The public was quick to follow suit, and George IV exclaimed: 'I have never heard anything to equal it, not only for perfect technique but for wealth of ideas. This boy surpasses Cramer and Moscheles.' Not for nothing did the King pride himself on being a connoisseur. Sébastien Érard had not wasted his time, either, for the English admired 'Érard's grand seven-octave pianoforte' which, combined with the young virtuoso, was quite an attraction.

Admidst all this fêting, the Liszts stayed on in London for the whole year, except for a visit to France during the summer. Despite this, serious work continued to make its demands upon Franz, as witness a letter from his father to Czerny: 'Putzi's one passion is for composition. His sonata for four hands, his trio and quintet would all delight you. He does two hours' practice a day with exercises, an hour of sight-reading and the rest of his time is devoted to composition. He has grown nearly as tall as me.' The most important work of all was on *Don Sanche*. This had been accepted in principle, but the score had still to be approved by a committee.

1825 Once the Christmas festivities were over, father and son returned to the Continent for a grand tour lasting two months. This was to take them, during February and March, to Marseilles, Lyons, Nîmes, Montpellier, Toulouse and Bordeaux. In April, Franz once again immersed himself in *Don Sanche* and he was in London again for the season from May to June, doing a tour of England. On 20 May he gave the first performance of a 'grand overture' at Manchester, which had no other name but which was in all probability that of *Don Sanche*.

Things then began to move rapidly. The Liszts returned to Paris in

July and on the 30th of that month Liszt presented his work to the management of the Opéra, whose verdict was favourable. On 11 August, the Ministry of Fine Arts ordered immediate production and the dress rehearsal took place on 15 October, with the first night on the 17th, after which there were to be only three more performances. The public reception was polite, even sympathetic, but extremely reserved. In the press there was on the one hand talk of a 'budding Mozart' and on the other a denial that he had the slightest talent for composition. To judge from the score, which can still be seen in the library of the Paris Opéra, the libretto was asine in the extreme and, despite some interesting musical ideas, the boy perhaps aimed rather high in tackling a form which requires considerable experience.

This same year, 1825, produced more of Liszt's first attempts in the field of composition, notably a *Tantum ergo,* a sonata for piano which for a time Liszt amused himself by passing off as an unknown work by Beethoven; an impromptu on themes by Spontini and Rossini; and a piano concerto. All these pieces are either lost or unpublished.

1826 These works have no more than a certain curiosity value, but there followed one which is of vastly more serious interest. This was *12 Études for Piano,* which was published in 1826 in Marseilles by Boisselot under the title *Études en 12 Exercises.* Reworked eleven years later, they became the notorious and vertiginous *Études d'exécution transcendante.*

Altogether, 1826 was a rather quiet year for Franz. He continued to work at counterpoint with Reicha, and it was not until the autumn that he set off on a tour of the provinces before going to Switzerland.

1827 The new year, in fact, found the father and son in Switzerland. It was to be a stormy year in every way. The young man, rather overworked, succumbed to great nervous fatigue. Doubtless as a result of this, he experienced a religious crisis. Sudden contempt overtook him for his profession as a virtuoso pianist and he thought about leaving it for the priesthood. He gave himself up to a life of prayer and asceticism, fasting to excess, with the result that his tiredness increased and he became sickly and prone to fainting fits and 'visions'. On the other hand, his reading of *The Desert Fathers, The Imitation of Christ, The Trappist* by Vigny and the *Odes* of Victor Hugo induced in him a state of ecstasy. Adam Liszt became desperate; there was nothing he could do, either by advice or by threats, to quieten Franz: 'You belong to art, not to the Church', he kept telling him, but with no effect.

The young man's state of health became more and more alarming and a rest cure at Boulogne-sur-Mer was prescribed. No sooner did they arrive there, however, than Adam Liszt fell ill. A violent gastric fever killed him in just a few days. He died on 27 August in the arms of his son, saying prophetically, as Liszt tells us: 'My child, I am about to leave you very much alone, but your talent will protect you against unforeseen circumstances. Your heart is good and you do not want for intelligence. But women make me frightened for you; they will disturb and dominate your life.'

Immediately after the funeral, which took place at Boulogne, Liszt, much shaken, returned to Paris where he joined his mother who had just arrived from Hungary, and the two moved into a small apartment at 7 bis Square Montholon. There Liszt resumed his life of mystical exaltation, spending hours in prayer at the nearby church of Saint-Vincent-de-Paul.

Little by little, however, he once again fell under the spell of Paris life. He was once more to be seen in the *salons*, where he was much sought after, and gave lessons to young society girls. It was in this way that he made the acquaintance of Caroline de Saint-Cricq. To have Liszt as one's teacher was the very last thing in chic, and the Comte de Saint-Cricq, Minister of Commerce and Manufacture in the Martignac Cabinet, summoned the young teacher, now something of a dandy, to be introduced to his daughter and to become her teacher. The two young innocents fell passionately in love at first sight, and the literature of the time did much to inflame the romance.

1828   It was in fact a most exalted and literary romance. Caroline's mother was tied to her bed by a serious illness and her father was often away from home. The lessons continued late into the night, with frenzied readings from Dante or Lamartine. The young woman was ravishingly beautiful, sixteen years of age and highly cultured. Liszt

17

Caroline de Saint-Cricq

gave her a ring on which he had had engraved the words: '*Expectans, expectavi*'. There was even a good deal of planning for the future; the almost dying Comtesse de Saint-Cricq was to some extent an accomplice and was imprudent enough to disclose these plans to her husband just before breathing her last: 'If they love each other, let them be happy,' she said. But Charles X's Minister was not so sentimental. No sooner was his wife dead than he summoned Franz, thanked him with icy courtesy, assured him of his esteem, settled his accounts and asked him never to return. Caroline thought she would go mad. She fell ill and wanted to retreat into a convent, but it was not long before her father took her in hand and married her to a minor nobleman from Béarn, the Comte d'Artigaux. Liszt was not to see the

Comtesse d'Artigaux again until 1844, and we shall see in what touching circumstances that meeting took place.

1829   After the dramas and crises of 1827 and the emotional upheavals of the previous year, Liszt was a broken man. He suffered another bout of depression, more serious this time, and became really ill. Some papers even went so far as to announce his death, and the reporter on *l'Étoile* wrote a eulogistic obituary.

At the same time Liszt went through another mystical crisis, rendered all the more acute by his disappointment in love. He spent all his time between his Confessor, the Abbé Bardin (who, like his father earlier on, did everything in his power to make him abandon his plans for the priesthood) and Christian Uhran, the first violin at the Opéra, who was so superstitiously religious that while he was in the orchestra pit he would keep his back to the stage in order to escape the wiles of the Devil. Once again, there were long prayers at Saint-Vincent-de-Paul, more fasting and ascetic practices. The whole of Paris followed the breakdown with an attention at the same time affectionate and indiscreet, and some very bad verses were published on the subject of his sufferings:

> *In vain are you silent, young lover!*
> *Your large, haggard eyes and hesitant step,*
> *Your deep-flushed cheek and faint, distant voice,*
> *All show you knew happiness once.*

1830   As with his previous crisis, however, Liszt quickly pulled himself out of his depression. Work and the company he kept contributed to his recovery. But it was nearly a year before he again ascended the concert platform from which he had been absent for many long months. This time, however, it was not love but literature which was to give him new life. Ideas were fermenting in his mind as a result of his ceaseless reading: *William Tell*, Montaigne, Voltaire, *Marion Delorme, René*, Sainte-Beuve, Lamartine, *Le Génie du Christianisme*, Senancour, Kant and, above all, Lamennais. The result of all this continuous reading, once absorbed and digested, was wild intellectual excitement. At about this time he became acquainted with Lamennais

19

and this made a deep impression on him, restoring all his passion for life. He no longer frequented only the society *salons* but also the artistic ones, where he met Berlioz, who introduced him to Goethe's *Faust,* a work which fired Franz's enthusiasm immediately.

But it was *Les Trois Glorieuses* that most of all inflamed this young 'right-wing' musician. Liszt and his mother had just left the Square Montholon for a larger apartment in the rue de Provence. Left-wing intellectuals are not an invention of our times. They had the same qualities, enthusiasms and touching naiveté then as now. During those passionate days when Paris was aflame and the July sun, itself particularly fiery, bore down on the capital, Liszt threw himself *con fuoco* into the composition of a Revolutionary Symphony dedicated to La Fayette. The symphony was never to be finished, but fragments of it appeared in later work (such as the *Marche Héroïque* and the *Héroïde funèbre*). In his mother's words 'he was cured by the canon'.

That autumn Liszt began playing concerts again and with singular

Lamennais by Guérin   *Liszt in 1830*

daring included the sonatas and even the concertos of Beethoven in his repertoire, a great risk in Paris, which was musically somewhat frivolous and where Beethoven's music was 'sneezed at' by the Director of the Conservatoire.

On 4 December Liszt visited Berlioz. It was the eve of the first performance of the *Symphonie fantastique*. There is no need to describe what happened the following evening; it has been done often enough. But Liszt was one of the most faithful supporters of *'Jeune France'*. He applauded madly and took Berlioz home to supper in the rue de Provence.

By 1830 *'le petit Litz'* had become a man.

MARCHE HONGROISE
d'Après Schubert

Lith Guillet

Pour Piano

F. LISZT.

✦ Prix 7f 50 ✦

Collection des Ouvrages de F. LISZT, Publiés par BERNARD-LATTE.

à Paris chez BERNARD-LATTE éditeur Boulevard des Italiens 2. Passage de l'Opéra.

Dear Marie, we are so necessary to
one another, *Franz*

Good-bye. I love you from the bottom of
my heart. May God guide you, *Marie*

THE TZIGANE

The year 1831 was to be relatively calm. Nothing outstanding
happened, at least on the strictly musical plane, except for a few tours
in France and Germany. In his enthusiasm for the *Symphonie
fantastique* Liszt had made an acrobatic transcription of it for piano
and had financed the publication himself, although he was at the time
the only one capable of executing it.

During his time in Paris he made the acquaintance of Mendelssohn
and Hiller, who were spending a few months there; more important
still, he met Félicien David, who introduced him to 'Saint-Simonism'.
Liszt's intellectual excitement reached an even higher pitch. In this
social religion, where he discovered the idea of the 'woman as redeemer'
and of 'social art' he found echoes of Lamennais' theories, which taught

23

Place de la Concorde in 1829 by Canell

that artistic regeneration meant social regeneration. Among the followers of Saint-Simon he rediscovered an atmosphere sympathetic to his priestly aspirations and his taste for the religious life. Moreover, he found that he was completely at one with his artistic vocation. All complications were swept away. He was in a state of perfect equilibrium.

1832 Although the previous year had not been rich in music, 1832 was quite different. The philosophic exaltation persisted, certainly, as it was to continue to his dying day, but 1832 was a year of great musical activity and discovery.

First of all on 9 March there was the first concert given by Paganini in Paris, at the Opéra. As a person, he irritated Liszt somewhat. The virtuoso in Paganini seemed to him to be decidedly suspect — and he should know. 'A monstrous self can only become a lonely, unhappy god', he wrote on this occasion. But he was fascinated from the technical point of view. And like Schumann, who was thinking along the same lines, Liszt believed that there could be a Paganini of the piano. Here was the essence of a great personal conflict. On 2 May he wrote to one of his pupils, Pierre Wolf:

'My mind and my fingers are working like the damned: Homer, the Bible, Plato, Locke, Byron, Hugo, Lamartine, Chateaubriand, Beethoven, Bach, Hummel, Mozart, Weber are all around me. I study them, meditate on them, devour them furiously. What is more, I work four or five hours at exercises (thirds, sixths, octaves, tremolos, repeated notes, cadenzas, etc). Oh, so long as I don't go mad, you'll rediscover an artist in me. Yes, the sort of artist you are looking for, the sort we need today. "I too am a painter!" cried Michelangelo the first time he saw a masterpiece . . . Small and poor as your friend is, he never stops repeating the words of the great man after hearing the last Paganini concert.'

At about this time, too, he discovered Chopin, when he came to play in Paris. The previous year Schumann had written his famous article entitled 'Hats off, gentlemen, a genius!' and just as Schumann was later on to dedicate his Fantasia to Liszt and the latter his Sonata to Schumann, so it was to Liszt that Chopin dedicated his first collection of Études. Such gifts, exchanged over the frontiers between people who hardly knew each other, were a delightful gesture.

The Chopin Études also prompted Liszt to rework his own youthful exercises and there emerged the *Études transcendantes*. His six Études, of which *La Campanella* was one, were inspired by the dazzling Paganini. Liszt, at the age of twenty-one, had already invented modern piano technique!

As a teacher, he worked miracles. 'An admirable lesson, admirable!' wrote Valérie Boissier (one of his pupils); 'I should have liked to write down every word from those twenty year old lips, one after the other.' She added, 'His organisation is quite different from that of other

Adèle de Laprunarède
by Guérin

mortals. Nature created it in an access of munificence.' It must also be said that his beauty created a great impression; the famous lithograph by Deveria published in that year bears witness to this.

Again, it was about this time that Liszt became aware of descriptive music: on 9 December at the Conservatoire he heard Berlioz's *Episode from the life of an artist, or the return to life* which paved the way for future symphonic poems.

 1833   During the course of the winter of 1832-33, Liszt had a new amorous adventure, which again set Paris talking. Though not positively committed to Saint-Simonism, he continued to be profoundly influenced by it. Dismissing the memory of Caroline, he fell in love with the Comtesse Adèle de Laprunarède. The brief adventure took place in a castle hidden away among the Alps. Cut off by snow, Franz and Adèle exchanged declarations of love under the absent-minded gaze of her senile husband.

About half-way through the year, however, during a surprise party organised by Heine, Delacroix and Mickiewicz at Chopin's house, Liszt made the acquaintance of Marie d'Agoult. A strong sympathy sprang up between them, which each tried hard to escape. Thanks to George Sand, they capitulated in the end, for she cleverly precipitated matters. But a tragic event was to bring them even closer together, although it seemed at first likely to separate them. This was the death of Louison, Marie's daughter, whom Liszt and the Comtesse d'Agoult had been nursing through a painful illness. Marie imagined it to be a punishment from God, but with a little philosophy and a great deal of passion, Franz managed to avoid a separation.

This period too is marked by great intellectual ferment. Liszt had numerous conversations with Lamennais and the Père Enfantin, and both exercised a deep influence on him. Lamennais was enthusiastic about the young man, in whom he saw the incarnation of one of his favourite images: the social artist-believer. Liszt on his side affirmed, curiously enough, that he was against art for art's sake. In the course of the copious correspondence he exchanged with Comtesse d'Agoult during these months, he developed these ideas. Soon he was writing:

'Let us hope that the artist of the future will renounce whole-heartedly the selfish, vain rôle which Paganini, as we believe, was the last to play, however illustriously. Let him aim at something not in himself, but outside himself; let virtuosity be a means, not an end, and let him always remember that as well as nobility, in fact probably more than nobility, genius obliges.'

In his passionate enthusiasm there are many contradictions and confusions, but to Heine, who reproached him for his 'weathervane' ideology, he replied:

'You accuse me of having a wavering character, and as proof you enumerate the many causes I have, according to you, embraced with ardour, the philosophical stables where I have in turn chosen my hobby-horses. But tell me, should not this accusation under which you are crushing me — and only me — be borne by our whole generation, if we are to be fair? . . . Are we not all rather wavering between a past we no longer want and a future we do not yet know? You yourself, with your noble mission as poet and thinker, have you always been quite able to discern the beams of your own star? This century is sick and we are all sick with it. The poor musician has still the smallest burden of responsibility, since he wields neither the pen nor the sword and can abandon himself without too much remorse to his intellectual curiosity and turn in any direction from which he sees light come.'

It was in 1833 that Liszt composed the *Pensées des morts*.

1834   Paris had accepted the love of Franz and Marie, but the latter was in torment. That spring, the woman whose literary *salon* had earned her the nickname of 'The Corinna of the Quai Malaquais' went to visit a fashionable pythoness, Mademoiselle Lenormant, who held court in a salubrious cavern in the rue de Tournon. She told Marie:

'There will soon be a total change in your destiny, and as a result you will even change your name. Your new name will become famous throughout Europe and you will leave your country for a long period. You will fall in love with a man who will enjoy sensational success. Distrust your imagination, which is easily stimulated and which will subject you to many dangers from which you will escape only by great courage.'

In the autumn Liszt retired for a while to stay with Lamennais at La Chênaie, which has been described as 'an oasis in the steppes of Britanny'. There followed much correspondence with Marie. He worked at a few theoretical studies and notably at an article on the ennoblement of religious music, which was published in the *Gazette Musicale*. It was a matter which was to preoccupy him — legitimately so in that century — to the end of his life.

Comtesse d'Agoult by Lehman

It was also in the autumn of 1834 that he composed the first piece of his collection entitled *Années de pèlerinage*. This was a piece called *Lyon,* inspired by the revolt of the workers there. At the top of the manuscript, the battle-cry of the rebels is inscribed as a sort of epigraph: 'Live working; die fighting.' The work is dedicated to M.F. de L.

 1835   On his return from his stay with Lamennais, Franz found Marie still in great agony of mind, battling with her conscience. The conflict between grief and love had made her thin and haggard.

At last the great decision was taken: in August, Liszt literally abducted the Countess. The lovers left for Switzerland accompanied by Marie's mother, a ruse designed to minimise the scandal. On 21 August they arrived in Geneva and moved into the Hotel des Balances. But the scandal had obviously broken, the mother, who could no longer be of any use, left soon afterwards for Paris, leaving them alone in a small apartment in the Rue Tabazan, at the corner of the Rue des Belles-Feuilles. From their windows they looked out over the magnificent panorama of the Salève and the Jura.

It was a period of great love and great labour. For Liszt, every other day was devoted to the piano, the alternate days being dedicated to fanatical reading in order to keep up with his companion. He attended lectures at the Academy, following Choisy's philosophy courses. Geneva society was obviously put out by this irregular, perceptive pair, but the lovers made a small circle of friends from whom Liszt was to learn a great deal of value. They included the botanist Pyrame de Candolle, the scientist Adolphe Pictet, the historian Simonde de Sismondi together with some friends of Chopin, Prince and Princess Belgiojoso and Countess Potocka.

Marie, infected by her companion's intellectual ardour, began to write (partly also because she was admittedly a little bored at Geneva). The two went on walks and longer outings in the vicinity, and some of the first fragments of the Swiss piano notebooks (*Années de pèlerinage*), notably *Au lac de Wallenstadt, Au bord d'une source* and *La Vallée d'Obermann,* took shape there. It was also at this time that Liszt composed his great study *De la situation des artistes,* partly to express his social preoccupations but also as a result of the worry he was experiencing by reason of his irregular association with Marie.

Lack of money was soon to call him back to more prosaic occupations. Liszt began to give concerts again. But (and this is typical of Liszt) most of them were charity concerts which brought him nothing. In the same way, although he was a professor at the Conservatoire, his courses were unpaid; so that he was forced to give private lessons in order to make a living. His notebooks about his pupils are charming.

'Julie Raffard: very remarkable feeling for music. Very small hands. Brilliant execution. Amélie Calame: Pretty fingers; works hard and carefully, almost too much so. Could teach. Marie Demellayer: Vicious technique (if technique there be), extreme zeal but little talent. Grimaces and contortions. Glory to God in the Highest and Peace to All Men of Good Will. Ida Miliquet: Swiss artist; flabby and mediocre. Quite good deportment at the piano. Jenny Gambini: beautiful eyes.'

Then, on 18 December, a happy event for the two lovers: the birth of their first daughter, Blandine. The same day, Liszt, in his enthusiasm, composed a new piece of the *Années de pèlerinage: Les Cloches de Genève,* which he dedicated to the child.

1836 Life went by tolerably peacefully. Franz was passionately attached to his daughter, whose birth, curiously enough, put many things right in the eyes of Geneva society, which now recognised the relationship.

When spring came they wrote to George Sand, urging her to join them on a trip to Chamonix. 'For six months,' Franz added, 'I have been doing nothing but write, scribble and scrawl notes of all colours and kinds. I am convinced that if one were to add them all up there would be several milliards. So I have become scandalously foolish and, as the proverb has it, as stupid as a musician.' But no-one really expected this friend from Paris to arrive, and so, accompanied by Pictet, now become the guide and mentor of the family, they left for the foot of Mont Blanc. At the beginning of September George Sand

Engraving from 'A Race in Chamonix: by Pictet.

and her two children arrived at Geneva. Finding no-one there, she hurried in pursuit of the Liszt family, whom she found at Chamonix. In the guest book at the Hotel de l'Union, Liszt had elaborated his entry poetically with the words: 'musician-philosopher, born on Parnassus, travelling from Doubt to Truth.' Not to be outdone, George Sand made a similar entry: '*Name of traveller:* Piffoëls and family. *Domicile:* Nature. *Travelling from:* God. *Destination:* Heaven. *Birthplace:* Europe. *Occupation:* loafers. *Date of documents:* Eternity. *Delivered by:* Public Opinion.'

They all lived as wildly as students, rather overwhelming the inhabitants of this hitherto peaceful spot. After the usual excursions, they left for Geneva via Freiburg, where Liszt played Mozart's *Dies Irae* on the Mooser organ in the cathedral.

But Liszt suddenly heard rumours of the success in Paris of the

Viennese pianist Thalberg. Cut to the quick, Liszt decided to make an immediate reappearance in France, whilst Marie, to avoid any difficulty with Paris society, went to live at Nohant with George Sand. Unfortunately, Liszt arrived too late to compete with Thalberg, who had already left the capital. He was shown the compositions which Thalberg had left behind him, and which some critics said were superior to Chopin's. Liszt thought they were bad, and hastened to say so in the *Revue Musicale.* So began a famous rivalry.

On 18 December Liszt once again presented himself to a Paris audience. The public was cold and in a bad mood. However, when Liszt started playing his own transcription of Berlioz's *Symphonie fantastique* it took only a few minutes for the hostile audience to thaw. They hailed the pianist with frenzied acclamations. Liszt had won the first round.

1837 However, in February Thalberg returned to Paris and gave a triumphant concert at the Théâtre Italien. Liszt at once took up the challenge and booked the Opéra, where he achieved a no less triumphant success. The final duel took place at the house of Princess Belgiojoso, where a joint recital brought the two pianists face to face. Thalberg played his fantasia on *Moïse* and Liszt his on *Niobe*. It is difficult to credit these days that the vanity of intelligent artists, combined with the cruelty of the public, could render such a competition possible. As a matter of fact, Liszt was not taken in, as is shown by what he wrote later: 'Because one man does not grant another the artistic merit that the masses seem to have exaggeratedly accorded him, are they necessarily enemies? They may well be reconciled by mutual appreciation and respect, apart from questions of art.' Epigrams abounded. One woman wrote: 'Thalberg is the best pianist in the world, but Liszt is the only one.' In fact, despite his conciliatory tone, Liszt rather shared the opinion of Chopin, who had declared: 'Thalberg plays excellently, but he is not the man for me. He plays his forte and piano with the pedal and not with his hands, plays tenths as easily as I play octaves and wears diamond shirt-buttons.'

One concert followed another during the winter of 1836-1837. Between tours, Liszt paid short visits to Nohant, where Marie was dying of boredom. The lovers' correspondence at this time included some of the best letters they ever wrote.

During a lull from May to July, Liszt actually went to live at Nohant, where George Sand had come to write *Mauprat*. She wrote in her diary:

'When Franz plays, I feel at peace. All my troubles become poetry, all my instincts become lofty. I love the interrupted phrases he throws on to the piano and which stay poised in mid-air. The leaves of the lime trees try to complete the melody. A powerful artist, sublime in great matters, always superior in small, but sad, and consumed with a secret wound. Fortunate man, loved by a beautiful and generous woman, intelligent and chaste as well, what more do you want, ungrateful creature? Oh, if only I were loved . . . '

Giorgia S . . . (anon.)

This, be it said, was the period when she had just finished with Musset. But the reign of Chopin was soon to begin.

It was during this stay at Nohant that Liszt composed his stupendous transcriptions of the Beethoven Symphonies for piano and his first arrangements of Schubert's Lieder.

In the company of a man as attractive and brilliant as he, relations between two women such as Marie and George Sand could hardly fail to become strained. Liszt noticed this and, as irritation of this kind was intolerable to him, he took Marie away. It was to be the last he saw of George Sand. These small difficulties heralded the break which was not long in coming and which, as a result, prevented Liszt and Chopin from enjoying a mutual feeling of friendship to the full.

In July Franz and Marie were at Lyons. After a charity concert they left for Mâcon, then for Saint-Point, where they visited Lamartine. One evening, Lamartine read aloud his *Bénédiction de Dieu dans la solitude* and Liszt sat down at the piano to play *Harmonies du soir,* which he had dedicated to the poet. After that it was Chambéry, then Bellagio on Lake Como, where they lived a life of passionate ecstasy – a second honeymoon. But there was hard work, too: Liszt composed the 'Dante' Sonata there and completely re-wrote the *Études d'exécution transcendante.*

On 25 December their second child, Cosima, was born.

Meanwhile Liszt, who spent the better part of his time giving concerts for the benefit of various charities, was never free from worry about his material situation. As it happened, Hummel had just died, leaving vacant the position of Director of Music at Weimar. Franz considered for a time trying this, but the irregularity of his situation prevented him from following the project through.

At the end of 1837, he wrote, for the *Gazette Musicale,* one of the first great articles in French on the music of Schumann, in which, with masterly perception, he demonstrated the importance of the great man's first piano works.

1838   By the early spring the family funds had run out. Franz resumed his concert tours, appearing first at La Scala, Milan, under the patronage of the House of Ricordi, in a city where the piano was not considered the highest form of art. Liszt, taking stock of people, situation and customs, improvised brilliant fantasies on themes suggested by the audience. Some of these themes were from fashionable composers such as Donizetti or Bellini; and some of them had very little to do with music at all. For instance, at his third Milan concert, he had to describe on the piano the famous Cathedral of Milan and, even more strange, he had to answer, on the piano, the question: 'Is it better to be married or to be a bachelor?' He played up to them, and was accepted by them. Then, using this acceptance, and his success with them, he was able to play to this Milan audience the Beethoven sonatas — a singularly daring move for those times.

This was a marvellous victory for Liszt, who was justly proud. But it was not enough. Such acrobatic feats began to depress him and leave him with a feeling of humiliation: 'Will the time for dedication and virile action never come? Am I condemned without remission to this occupation of buffoon and jester to the salons?' he wrote to Lamennais.

He went on to Venice, where the frivolity of the public brought his despair to rock bottom. He left Marie there and departed forthwith to Vienna where he applied himself eagerly to playing for the Hungarian victims of the Danube floods. Engaged for two concerts, he gave ten in one month. In this there was one great consolation for him: after Italy, what a serious public! His visit left him with a great feeling of achievement, enabling him to send 25,000 guilders to Hungary. He played at Court and was received with pleasure. The *Soirées de Vienne* were composed and the two collections of Schubert Lieder transcriptions finished. He was able to bring to the public the latest works of Chopin and Schumann. He discovered Schumann's *Carnaval* and the *Phantasiestücke* and, above all, made the acquaintance and succumbed to the attraction of Clara Wieck. Schumann's wife-to-be certainly shared this feeling, although Liszt's rich and stormy nature rather shook her *petit-bourgeois* way of life. Clara wrote in her diary:

'We heard Liszt. He can be compared to no other virtuoso — he is unique of his kind. He inspires fear and astonishment, and is a very likeable artist. His posture at the piano cannot be described — it is all his own. He gives himself up to it. His passion is limitless. Often he offends the sense of beauty by tearing at the melody. His spirit is huge. It is true to say that his art is his life.'

Quite a pretty compliment.

Liszt wanted to take advantage of being in Vienna to proceed to his mother country, but a letter from Marie, who was ill in Venice, called him back. On the night of his departure all his friends, musicians and gentlefolk alike (Czerny and Clara among them), held a magnificent party for him and accompanied him joyfully and ceremoniously to the coach.

Once back with Marie, he took her to convalesce in Lugano. Despite his success in Milan, Liszt had rather bad memories of this adventure, and had in the meantime sent the Paris *Gazette Musicale* a lively article on La Scala and Italian music. The Italian critics immediately rose up against him. Three important Italian journals published articles entitled: *'Guerra al F.Liszt'*. From Lugano, he sent this reply to the three editors:

'Dear Sir, Invective and insults continue to flow from the papers. As I have already said, I am not going to involve myself in a battle of words. To judge from the tone of the *Pirate* and the *Theatre Courier* this could only be an exchange of offensive remarks. Still less can I reply to anonymous insults. I therefore wish to declare, for the hundredth and last time, that my intention was never to outrage Milan society. I also declare that I am prepared to offer the necessary explanation to anyone who may ask it of me. Friday morning, 20 July.'

This said, he left for Milan and, after having driven around the town ostentatiously in an open carriage, he installed himself in the foyer of his hotel to await the reaction. None came.

This Italian skirmish did not, however, leave him with any distaste for the country. Moreover, a series of concerts awaited him there, and he remained in Italy until the end of the year, playing at Modena, Florence and Bologna in particular, and also taking the opportunity to visit churches and museums with Marie.

1839 At the end of January the family settled in Rome, in the Via della Purificazione, for about ten months. Although Marie's presence and mood sometimes seemed to weigh on him rather irritatingly, Liszt was enchanted with the place. He wrote:

'Beauty, in this privileged country, appeared to me in its purest and sublimest forms. Art revealed itself before my eyes in all its splendour; its universality and unity were disclosed to me. Each day brought home to me more and more the hidden connections uniting works of genius. Raphael and Michelangelo gave me a better understanding of Mozart and Beethoven. Giovanni da Pisa, Fra Beato and Francia explained to me Allegri, Marcello, Palestrina. Titian and Rossini appeared to me like two heavenly bodies shining with the same light. The Colosseum and the Campo Santo are not so different as one might think from the 'Eroica' Symphony and the Requiem. Dante has found his pictorial expression in Orcagna and Michelangelo. One day no doubt he will find his musical expression in the Beethoven of the future.'

These lines are taken from one of the *Letters from a bachelor of music* dedicated to Berlioz and dated 2 October 1839.

During this period Liszt completed his *Années de pèlerinage* and composed some of the most important pieces of his two Italian notebooks, notably the three *Sonetti del Petrarca, Il Penseroso* and *Sposalizio,* all of which incorporate many impressions gained outside Rome, for Liszt and Marie travelled a great deal that year.

It was during this period that Liszt took up with Ingres, then Director of the *École de Rome.* And it is thanks to the composer that we know, from a fairly reliable source, that the famous *'violon d'Ingres'* was not a joke. Liszt, who had played Beethoven's Sonata in A minor with him, wrote:

'Ah, if you had only heard him then! The religious fidelity with which he plays Beethoven's music! How firm and full of warmth is his bowing! How pure his style, how true his feeling! Despite the respect I feel for him I could not help but throw my arms about him, and was happy to feel him press me to his breast with paternal tenderness.'

But clouds were gathering over the Liszt household. Notwithstanding the birth of a third child, Daniel, a certain tension had sprung up between the two. Marie, very feminine and rather a blue-stocking, had not kept up with Franz's development. And this applied not only in the intellectual sphere, where she could dominate, but rather in relation to the whole flowering of his genius. She would put on airs in front of unwilling listeners and talk pretentious nonsense, comparing herself over-readily with the great inspirers of history. At one time Louis de Ronchaud was present at a conversation during the course of which Liszt, no doubt provoked, let fall a rash remark. Marie had encouraged Ronchaud to defend her point of view and he had observed: 'She is right. Woman is man's inspiration. Think of Dante and Beatrice!' To which Liszt had replied: 'It is the Dantes of this world who make the Beatrices — and the real ones die at eighteen!' True, this was tit for tat, for on another occasion Marie had called him a 'trumped-up Don Juan'. Like many of his friends, she held his career against him, a profound mistake to make with a man who was the first to suffer from it, and who had already explained his position in this respect to Pictet: 'My piano is to me what a ship is to a sailor, or a horse to an Arab. More, perhaps, because my piano has hitherto been my speech, my life; it is the intimate repository of everything that has been going on in my mind during the most passionate days of my youth. All my desires, all my dreams, all my joys and sorrows are there.' And now there was a woman and three children . . .

His courtesy exhausted, Liszt sent everybody back to Paris in November to stay with his mother, while he resumed his life of travelling virtuoso. Faithful to the principle of incorrigible contradiction which marked his whole career, this man who played the piano to earn a living began by giving a whole series of concerts which brought him nothing but glory. This was the affair of the Beethoven memorial at Bonn. A fund had been established and had yielded, in France, 424.90 francs. Liszt was violently and justifiably angry with his adopted country. He at once wrote to Bonn to announce that he was going to give some concerts, and guaranteed 60,000 francs. Between 18 November and 4 December he gave six concerts in Vienna. They were a triumph in every way. He then went to play at Pressburg where, twenty years earlier, he had made his first public appearance. On 21 December he made a spectacular entry into Pest, where he had been invited, and was greeted as a national hero. He received the hospitality of the Count Leo Festetics and gave a number of concerts to wildly enthusiastic houses.

1840 The day after the New Year celebrations, he mounted the platform again at Pest. On 2, 4, 8, 9 and 11 January, he gave more concerts. On one occasion he provoked a veritable musical and patriotic delirium by improvising a brilliant transcription of the 'Rakoczy' March, which he was to take up again in one of his Rhapsodies. A sword of honour was presented to him and he received the diploma of Citizen of Honour of Pest before thousands of fellow citizens acclaiming him: *'Eljen Liszt Ferencz!'*

Tearing himself away, not without regret, from these festivities, he called at Oedenburg, where he gave several more concerts for charity, and finally arrived at Raiding, the village where he was born. Here he enjoyed a magnificent welcome, amidst great celebration. With equal generosity he distributed money to all the poor throughout the course of this great municipal fête. It was now that he began to compose his Fantasia on Hungarian Folk Tunes, his symphonic poem 'Hungaria' and his Rhapsodies.

He played in Prague and Dresden with the same success. On the other hand, on 17 March in Leipzig, that most conservative of cities, he suffered the most brutal set-back. There was even some whistling after his performance of Beethoven's 'Pastoral' Symphony. Liszt had been spoiled by his audiences up to now and he took the blow badly. He took to his bed in despair and cancelled all other concerts. Schumann, Mendelssohn and Hiller rallied round him, visited him and tried to console him, to such effect that he decided to give a second concert after all, during which he did in fact manage to unfreeze this audience whose hostility stemmed more from tradition and a sort of local snobbery than from any true conviction. He did this with a dazzling interpretation of Weber's *Konzertstück*, a work which had itself been greeted with whistles at its first performance in Leipzig.

It was at this time that he became intimately acquainted with

Presentation of a sword of honour to Liszt on the stage of the Budapest Theatre, 1840.

Schumann. Schumann, like Clara, was somewhat put off by Liszt's rather actorish, even flashy, appearance, and in two letters to Clara dated 18 and 20 May he wrote:

'I have never heard anyone play so boldly, almost wildly . . . Clara, this is not my style; I would not give the art you practise for all the splendour of his playing, in which I detect a hint of showiness. . . . He is truly extraordinary, but do not model yourself on him, my Clara Wieck, just stay as you are. . . . Liszt seems to me to increase daily in stature and power. . . . He played me the *Noveletten* a fragment of the *Phantasiestücke* — the sonata — and I was stunned. He does many things which differ from my way of thinking, but they always have genius.'

Liszt continued his wanderings through Europe: London, Hamburg, Brussels, Baden, Frankfurt, Bonn. Everywhere he went he inspired wonder. Yet, as a pianist, he was constantly innovating. And this is something to be stressed. During these tours, he was the daring innovator of many ideas which we now take for granted, but which were amazing at the time. He was the first pianist to play without a score, the first to give a solo piano recital. Moreover, he was the first to devote a recital to a single composer (and those he chose were at the time not always accepted by the general public, for example Beethoven and Schumann). In short, it was Liszt who at that time invented the pattern of the modern recital.

Finally, in the autumn of the year 1840, there occurred a meeting which was to be of considerable importance in the history of music: a

Wagner by Ernest Kietz

young German musician, unknown and rather poor, came to ask him for help. His name was Richard Wagner. This first contact took place in a house in the Rue Casimir-Périer in Paris. The two men were not to see each other again for four years.

1841   No sooner were the New Year festivities over than Franz took his leave. First of all to Scotland, then in February to Belgium, and finally to England. This last visit was not particularly fortunate. The public was luke-warm or sullen. Moreover, Marie d'Agoult, who was now keeping a very watchful eye on him, forced her presence upon him so oppressively that the pianist seems to have become exasperated with her importunities. In the spring and early summer, success returned with concerts at Hamburg, Kiel and Copenhagen.

For the holidays, the whole family repaired to the island of Nonnenwerth on the Rhine. There followed a period of rest and reading. His imagination fired by this land of legend, Liszt immersed himself in German literature and poetry, devouring the work of Heine, Goethe, Schiller and Uhland. They made trips to the surrounding country and from time to time they all visited Cologne, where the unfinished Cathedral was a source of great interest: 'I do not know why it is,' wrote Liszt, 'that the sight of a cathedral moves me strangely. Is it because music is the architecture of sound, or architecture crystallised music? I do not know, but there certainly exists between these two arts a close relationship. I shall give my artist's mite towards the completion of the Dom.'

Then in November came separation again. Marie went back to Paris with the children and Liszt left again for a journey across Europe. In November he was splendidly received at the Court of Weimar, leaving for Leipzig in December and staying finally in Berlin, where he gave twenty-one concerts.

1842   During his stay in Berlin, Liszt enjoyed the most triumphant demonstrations of popularity. His success was at its height. Every sort of honour was conferred on him. The future Abbé was admitted to the Royal York Masonic Lodge, a much sought after distinction. As his knowledge of Germany deepened, so his natural love of the country

43

strengthened. In his letters he praises all the various beauties to be found in the 'land of the symphony'.

But his life in Berlin was not taken up solely with professional matters. Personal considerations played a great part and there was in particular what a contemporary described as 'an attractive feminine distraction' in the person of the great tragedienne Charlotte de Hagn, who wrote him poems:

> Poet, hide not from me what is love.
> Love is the soft breath of your tender soul.
> Poet, teach me the meaning of a kiss.
> The shorter the kiss the greater is your sin.

Charlotte spoke French marvellously and Liszt did not hesitate to put these drawing-room verses to music. He must have made a singular impression on the actress for, some years later, she wrote to him: 'You have spoiled me for all other men; no other can stand comparison. You are and remain unique.' But Liszt was not satisfied with this. If he inspired this sort of sentiment, he was also prone to very strong feelings himself and when he met the extraordinary woman, Bettina von Arnim, friend of Goethe and Beethoven and then aged fifty-seven, he struck up a strange amorous friendship with her. She, being somewhat of an expert on great men, immediately detected in Liszt an exceptional being. Liszt on his side was fascinated by the frail, thoughtful, if over-bearing woman. He listened passionately to her and read with no less devotion the numerous notes she wrote him:

'Whatever chord you touch in me, you awaken in me the need to better myself, the desire for effort which is aroused by the first wonderment of life. To be an artist, what is it if not to feel the first wonderment of life. To be an artist, what is it if not to feel time ripening within oneself? What is the sign that decks your way? It is youth. May it be the sole mediator of your immortality. Enthusiasm is nothing if it does not defend man's security, if it does not become the living source of health. . . . You who steep your head in the sources of harmony, what else could give you hope but nature, that daughter of heaven and earth? You must capture the spirit of the world. You must deafen it . . . You know well enough that of those who have fêted you, there are few who have understood you. But youth has sensed the holy ardour of your genius. I wish you well. I love you. Time has showered me with its fertilising rain. In me there are germinating and shooting the hidden seeds of the highest will. Rejoice. Ask nothing more of destiny than the power to open out to youth the enchanted world of heroes.'

It is agreeable to receive such letters when one is about thirty, particularly from a woman who has said similar things to Goethe and Beethoven. But it will have been noticed by now that the majority of women Liszt loved were argumentative, with literary and philosophical inclinations. The style was typical of the times, and he liked it.

After Berlin and all these various triumphs, Liszt arrived in Koenigsberg, where he was greeted with the same ceremony by the musical world and was made a Doctor *honoris causa*. In the spring he made a tour of Russia and took up residence for a while in Saint Petersburg.

That summer, as in the previous year, the family stayed at Nonnenwerth, and things were rather dismal. In September, Liszt made a short journey to Weimar, where he was more and more in demand at Court and where he was to be appointed *Kapellmeister* the following November. Liszt thus took upon himself functions which were not in fact fulfilled until two years later. These were defined in a document drawn up over the signature of the Theatre Intendant:

'Liszt will spend three months here each year, that is September and October, or October and November, as well as the month of February.

I. For the concerts he will be arranging he wishes to have the right to direct the orchestra, without prejudice to the position of M. Chélard, who will direct it on all other occasions.

II. Monsieur Liszt wishes to remain Monsieur Liszt for his lifetime, not accepting any other title.

III. As to payment, Monsieur Liszt will be content with any sum which it may be deemed suitable to grant him for his services during these three months.

Written after my conversation with Monsieur Liszt on 30 October 1842. Monsieur Liszt informed me today that he will accept with gratitude and pleasure the title *of Kapellmeister* for special service.'

1843 A working year without any outstanding events. Tireless concert tours in Germany, Russia and Poland and in the summer, another holiday at Nonnenwerth. Marie's mood had not improved. It should be said that during their later travels Liszt had already unleashed a stream of rumours by his passing *amours* with a tumultuous and seductive train of beautiful admirers. It is curious rather than of any direct consequence, to note that it was during this same year that Liszt composed a song entitled *Jeanne d'Arc au bûcher,* based on a poem by Alexandre Dumas.

1844 As the New Year approached, travels began again. Liszt was at that time giving innumerable concerts, particularly in Germany. He stopped off at Dresden simply in order to attend a performance of *Rienzi* and, wishing to congratulate Wagner, found him mistrustful and aloof. Again the encounter was only brief. It should be added that Liszt was once more travelling with a female retinue which was causing quite a stir, the most notable among them being the Irish-Andalusian Lola Montès, whose beauty was as celebrated as her eccentricity. This kind of commotion did not appeal to Wagner, but in any case Liszt did not allow himself to be pursued for long by this attractive but excitable lady. News of the affair had, however, already travelled and Marie d'Agoult was to make use of it to end a situation which was becoming more false every day. This was breaking point and it was, for Franz, a great relief. For Marie, it heralded a period of rather surprising hatred and vengefulness. Back in Paris society, she began to write in order to relieve her fury. Liszt's companions had always wielded an abundantly flowing pen and Marie transformed herself for the occasion into a poet, addressing her farewells to the composer in verse form:

Lola Montès, 1844.

No, you shall not hear from her too proud lips
One reproach, one regret in the searing farewell
No sorrow, no remorse for your fickle soul
In this silent adieu.
You will think that she too, drunk with empty fame
And the tears of yesterday, forgetting all tomorrow,
She, too, has broken faith with a mocking smile
And gone upon her way
And you will never know that, faithful and unrelenting
She is departing on a dark voyage from which there is no return
And in fleeing the lover, carries love with her into eternal night.

Marie was not gifted poetically, and we shall see later how her fury was to inspire her on the literary level.

All this did not prevent Liszt from showing up in Paris, where he gave two dazzling concerts on 16 and 25 April at the Théâtre Italien. Then there were fresh concert tours, bread-and-butter ones this time, for he had to ensure his children's education, which was still in the luxury class. He visited the great cities of France and, on one such occasion, at Pau, met the object of his first love, Caroline de Saint-Cricq, now Madame d'Artigaux. He immediately composed for her the song: *Ich möchte hingehen wie das Abendroth*, based on a poem by George Herwegh. On the manuscript, he wrote the following dedication: 'This song is the testament of my youth.'

 1845   Liszt now became obsessed with the idea of establishing a stable mode of life. His virtuoso's existence seemed empty to him, but he still pursued it. That year there were to be tours in Spain and Portugal, and in August he found himself once again in Germany. At last, the monument to Beethoven, to which he had so generously subscribed, was to be inaugurated. In fact, he contributed a good deal more money, to ensure that the celebrations should be worthy of it. He also cooperated by conducting the Symphony in C minor and the Finale of *Fidelio*, and by playing the E flat Concerto. His own *Festkantate* was also performed. It had been written for the occasion, but suffered badly in execution. Without waiting for the polite applause which was in any case slow to come, Liszt played an encore quickly and all was well.

 1846   In February Liszt, who had now taken up his functions as *Kapellmeister* at Weimar, returned to direct the Grand-Ducal orchestra, afterwards resuming his route through Austria, Hungary and the Danube Principalities to Russia.

This was the year when Marie d'Agoult, under the pen name of Daniel Stern, published her first novel of revenge: *Nélida*, in which the author depicts herself in an extremely flattering light and Liszt becomes a painter-cad, devoured with remorse for having deceived the one he loved, and eventually dying repentant. It is also worth noting that Liszt consistently refused to recognise himself in this hate-ridden, rancorous and talentless work, although the allusions contained in it are unconcealed.

> Believe me, Carolyne, I should be as mad as
> Romeo if I thought that he was mad. *Franz*

> May the Angel of the Lord guide you, you who
> are my radiant morning star. *Carolyne*

'NEL MEZZO DEL CAMMIN DI NOSTRA VITA . . . '

The year 1847 was to mark a turning point in the life of Liszt. The wandering virtuoso was dreaming ceaselessly of another way of life. He wrote to the Grand Duke Charles Alexander of Saxony: 'The moment is coming (*nel mezzo del cammin di nostra vita*) to break out of my virtuoso's chrysalis and let my thought fly free. . . . My first and paramount aim just now is to conquer the theatre with my thought, just as I have conquered it over the past years with my artistic personality.'

Nevertheless, it was through playing the pianistic fool once again that he was to find his road to Damascus. In February, he was on tour in Kiev and at one of his concerts an impassioned member of the audience, having heard Liszt's *Pater noster* at Mass, had paid the

lla d'Este

Princess Carolyne a
her daughter (in r
style of Casano

exorbitant sum of a hundred roubles for her ticket, for the house was sold out. She sought an introduction to Liszt, looked deep into his eyes and, a few months later, our apostle of masculine liberty found himself holidaying with his new captor, a small, swarthy woman, Jeanne Elisabeth Carolyne Iwanowska, Princess Nicolas de Sayn-Wittgenstein, whose lands were situated in Southern Russia, at Woronince.

The holiday lasted throughout the autumn and winter. Once again Liszt had fallen for a woman with a literary-philosophical turn of mind whom he was later to refer to as 'my mystic amazon'. Carolyne, eigh years younger than Liszt, was quite a sportswoman, who could stay ir the saddle for eight hours at a stretch. She was a devout Roma

Catholic, although she had originally been orthodox. An aristocrat with social inclinations, she was a person of considerable culture, but at least at that time, passionate rather than intellectual. She was not pretty but Liszt, hitherto the tireless lover of beautiful women, was fascinated by her. During these months alone together, they philosophised endlessly and with this strange creature the composer rediscovered the spiritual exaltation he had known throughout his youth. The lofty pre-occupations of the Princess were to serve only to crystallise his artistic desires and he finally decided to abandon the exhausting and futile life of the virtuoso to aim at higher art. It was during his stay at Woronince that he was to sketch the 'Dante' Symphony, the *Harmonies poétiques et religieuses* and *Ce qu'on entend sur la montagne.* He hoped to set himself up permanently at Weimar, and the Princess decided to secure an annulment of her marriage in order to marry Liszt.

A few phrases taken from her letters provide the tone of their relationship:

'I cannot take any step except towards you and with you — All my faith, all my hope and all my love are concentrated and summed up in you — *et nunc et semper* — Ineffable secrets have been revealed to me in you and now I can die in peace, blessing your name . . . I understand only two things: work and the fifth chapter of *The Imitation of Christ'.* . . . Oh, I must see you again soon, for all my heart and soul, faith and hope, are in you, through you and for you. May the Angel of the Lord guide you, you who are my radiant morning star!'

Liszt is not to be outdone, and his ardour has the same intensity: 'Believe me, Carolyne, I should be as made as Romeo, if I thought that he was mad . . . To praise you, to love you, simply to give you pleasure, I shall try to achieve what is beautiful and new . . . I believe in love through you, in you and with you. Without this love I want neither earth nor heaven. . . . Let us love each other, my unique and glorious beloved, in God and in our Lord Jesus Christ, and let no man put asunder those whom God has joined together for eternity.'

1848   Now began one of the most fertile periods of Liszt's career. He was at last to find the life's ideal which he had sought so long and so fervently.

The decision was taken: they were to go to Weimar. Apparently decisive matrimonial plans were laid, for Carolyne thought she would easily find the support she needed for her annulment at the Court of the Tsar and the Grand Duchess Maria-Pavlovna. Despite her hopes, however, the outlook began to seem dismal. Revolution had begun to reverberate throughout Europe. Frontiers were more or less closed. It was difficult for the fleeing Princess to settle her personal affairs. In the meantime, Liszt had had to leave for Germany. In April, the two lovers rejoined each other in Austria, in a chateau belonging to the Prince Lichnowsky. Carolyne insisted upon a visit to Raiding and Eisenstadt and finally they left for Weimar where they settled at the Altenburg. From then on, the couple were celebrities all over Europe and a ceaseless flow of cosmopolitan society, elegant and artistic, converged upon the Altenburg, crowding round the prodigious creative genius who had shown himself to be at the same time composer, musical director, *Kapellmeister,* teacher and author. The influence of the masculine woman on the feminine man was excellent. The virtuoso and the tourist of the *Années de pèlerinage* disappeared to make way for the thinker and composer of the symphonic poems. Already during his stay at Prince Lichnowsky's chateau he had finished his 'Hungaria', and he was now inclining towards the composition of large-scale works. The following thirteen years were filled with creative activity. The story of his life was to become simply the story of the music he was composing and interpreting, as he led the sedentary life of a sort of musical pope.

Wagner reappeared in Liszt's life this year. Up until then, relations between the two artists had been confined to the two brief encounters previously described, and to four letters written at yearly intervals. On 23 June Wagner inaugurated the voluminous file of incessant demands which he was to press upon Liszt in a most curious correspondence. The letter of 23 June opened as follows: 'Excellent friend – you told me recently that you had closed your piano for a while; I imagine therefore that you have turned banker for the time being. I am in an unfortunate situation, and it has just occurred to me that you might

54

come to my rescue. . . .' One of the most beautiful friendships in the history of music was born, and was to develop, crescendo, until the celebrated avowal: 'One single chord brings us nearer together than all the words in the world:

Continue to love me as I love you, wholeheartedly.' (Liszt to Wagner)

1849   This year Liszt produced successively: *Tasso, Lamento e Trionfo,* taken from Byron, which was to have its first performance under the direction of Liszt on 1 August; *Ce qu'on entend sur la montagne,* taken from Victor Hugo, first performed the following February; the dithyramb *Weimar's Todten,* performed on 29 August; and the *Heroïde funèbre,* taken by the composer from his draft for the 'Revolutionary' Symphony of 1830.

But, as always at Weimar, Liszt was thinking of others. This year, it was to be Wagner. He directed a triumphal performance of *Tannhäuser* at which, as it happened, Wagner was unable to be present.

1850   This was the year of *Mazeppa* taken from Victor Hugo, and of *Prometheus* taken from Herder. These works, like the preceding ones, were dedicated to the Princess of Sayn-Wittgenstein; then came a *Concerto pathétique* and *Puissance de la musique.* And again it was Wagner who was to benefit by Liszt's initiative in arranging a production of *Lohengrin.*

1851   Plans for marriage with the Princess seemed to be nearing completion and Liszt decided to celebrate the hoped-for event by composing a new symphonic poem, a sort of epithalamium, entitled *Festklänge.* He also wrote that curious work called Fantasia and Fugue on the Choral *Ad nos, ad salutarem undam* for organ, on a theme from Meyerbeer's *Le Prophète.* The score is dedicated to Meyerbeer.

1852   Liszt spent this year doing various things at once and preparing future works, finishing nothing of importance. On the other hand, in March he directed a production of Berlioz's *Benvenuto Cellini,* an outstanding success which consoled the composer for the setback he had suffered in Paris at the time of its first performance.

1853 A great year. Liszt embarked on the 'Faust' Symphony, finished *Orpheus,* composed *An die Künstler,* but above all put the finishing touches to a masterpiece which was not only to remain unique in his work but was to be unique in the history of music, a score of staggering originality and inspiration, whose bold free construction sums up Liszt's entire genius: the Piano Sonata. This first attempt, a master stroke, was dedicated to Robert Schumann.

That autumn Liszt and the Princess paid a visit to Paris, where Liszt joined his three children, whom he had not seen for a very long time. Wagner was also there, and the two tall girls, aged respectively eight and fifteen years, were introduced to him. It would be interesting to know what he thought of Cosima then, who was later to become his wife.

There were frequent visits to Berlioz, who was living in extremely difficult circumstances and whose wife was dying.

Then Liszt returned to Weimar, where he was to take up his duties at

Drawing by Frédéric Preller

Cosima   Blandine   Daniel

the theatre. The music of Wagner was still to take up most of his attention during that season. 'On New Year's Day', he wrote to Wagner, 'we shall have here *The Flying Dutchman*. The last two performances of *Tannhäuser* have consecrated Weimar as your official stage. Without flattering ourselves, I doubt whether your work has up to now been performed so satisfactorily.' The friendship between Liszt and Wagner was expressed in correspondence in extremely lyrical terms. 'Thanks, oh my beloved Christ, my First Noël!' replied Wagner. 'I think of you as the Saviour himself and as such I have placed your image on the altar of my work!'

1854   This was another fertile year. Liszt finished the 'Faust' Symphony dedicated to Berlioz, reworked *Les Préludes,* a symphonic poem after Lamartine, for which the sketch of 1848 served as introduction to a great choral work entitled *Les quatre éléments* (an unpublished work composed around a poem by Joseph Autran and performed only twice, at Marseilles). It was on 28 February that Liszt conducted, at Weimar, the first performance of this famous score. This was also the year in which he undertook the composition of his great organ work Fantasy and Fugue on the name of B.A.C.H.

All this time, Liszt didn't forget his other friends. He put on a production of Schubert's *Alfonso und Estrella* at the Weimar theatre, but it was primarily Wagner and his music which accounted for the greater part of Liszt's activity. The correspondence between the two men this year was particularly representative of their close friendship, as also of Liszt's tireless dedication.

He writes:

'My very dear Richard, What a destiny is ours! To be obliged to live apart from one another like this! All I can say to you is that I think of you ceaselessly and love you from the bottom of my heart. It has been difficult for me recently, busy as I am with travelling and work, etc. But let us leave aside these details and talk about the *Rheingold*. Have you really finished it? You have worked extraordinarily quickly. You know what a joy it will be to me to see the score. Send it to me as soon as you can spare it. In the meantime, I have not neglected your financial affairs, and I trust my hopes will not be disappointed. Answer me sincerely on these two points:

1. Have you any debts which are worrying you? And what sum is absolutely necessary to pay them off?

2. Will you be unable to get out of difficulty again this year with your earnings?'

But, in another letter, Liszt also confided to Wagner:

'My only friend, I am often very sad on your account, and have no cause to be happy about myself. The principal concern and problem of my social life is taking a very serious and painful turn. I could hardly expect anything else from that quarter, and I am prepared for it, but the interminable complications I am obliged to deal with have entailed a great deal of worry for me and have seriously compromised my financial situation, so much so that I am at the moment unable to come to the aid of a friend. . . . I am very tired, and have very little energy. But spring will give us new strength . . . '

Meanwhile, the Princess was comforting everyone and urging them all to work. It was on account of her that Berlioz wrote *Les Troyens* and Wagner persisted with *The Ring*. And although she would jokingly refer to Liszt as her 'lazybones', she acknowledged the value of his activities. She wrote to Wagner:

'How good he is, how intelligent, tactful and patient he is, no-one knows this better than I! Any other man would have gone under and drowned a dozen or more times these last six years with the storms that have belaboured our poor little boat! But he somehow makes us weather them! Liszt has written to Berlin to find you someone to copy your *Rheingold,* the beautiful *Rheingold* we are all ears to hear. The person he hoped would do for you will not be free for a time. What is to stop you beginning the *Valkyrie?* and that admirable scene between Wotan and Brünnhilde. . . . Do that, get on with your *Valkyrie* as quickly as you can!'

1855   The difficulties Liszt referred to in his letter to Wagner were those occasioned by the Princess's demands for an annulment. This was slow in coming from Rome on account of the intrigues instigated by some of the members of her family, and by some of the Russian court. Liszt had rejoiced rather too soon when, some years earlier, he had composed his symphonic poem *Festklänge* to celebrate the joy of a union he believed to be imminent. And it was in 1854, just as the bad news arrived from Rome, that he conducted the first performance of his work.

He was not to be defeated, however, and plunged himself into a non-stop programme of work. Having, so to speak, sung his worries by putting to music the thirteenth psalm ('Eternel, jusques à quand m'oublieras-tu sans cesse?') he resumed work on the 'Dante' Symphony which he had started at the beginning of his association with the Princess. He wrote the 'Gran' Mass (Graner Messe) and on 16 February at Weimar, under the direction of Berlioz, he gave the first performance of his Concerto in E flat. After this he put on Schumann's *Genoveva* in April and at his concerts gave performances of all the newest works.

All the time, he continued to teach. The great pianists of the day came to consult him. His instruction was not limited to the piano: with his miraculous versatility, he also gave courses in the organ, harp and even the trombone.

Nor had he abandoned his literary work (the Princess certainly took an active part in this) and he completed his work on Chopin, worked on *Des Bohémiens et de leur musique en Hongrie* and sent numerous articles to French and German magazines on new works of music. All this time, the correspondence with Wagner continued, more intense and voluminous than ever.

In August, learning that Marie d'Agoult was no longer taking proper care of her daughters, he sent for them to come to the Altenburg. They remained there until September, when the mother of one of Liszt's young pupils, Hans von Bülow, took them to Berlin to give them a musical education and in particular to teach them the importance of defending 'the music of the future'.

Some time later, Liszt had the following report from Bülow:

'You ask me, my very dear Master, to give you news of mes-demoiselles Liszt. Until now, this would have been impossible in view of the state of astonishment, admiration and even exaltation into which they had thrown me, especially the younger one. As to their gift for music, this is not a talent, it is a genius. . . . Last evening, Mlle Bladine played the Sonata in A by Bach, and Mlle Cosima the Sonata in E flat of Beethoven. I am also putting them to work on piano arrangements of instrumental works for four hands. I make them analyse them, and am perhaps paying too much, rather than too little, attention to the supervision of their studies. . . . I shall never forget the delightful evening when I played your Psalm to them over and over again. Both these angels were as if kneeling in adoration of their father. They understand your masterpieces better than anyone and indeed you have a natural audience in them. How moved and touched I was to recognise you in Mlle Cosima's playing, *ipsissimum Lisztum.* . . .'

 1856   Worries and difficulties continued: Liszt wrote again to Wagner to express regret at the renewed delay in being able to help him:

'I have told you at various times of the financial difficulties of my situation. This is it, in all its simplicity: my mother and my three children are suitably provided for, thanks to my earlier savings. As for me, I am obliged to make do with my salary as *Kapellmeister* (1,000 thalers a year, plus 300 thalers as a grant for performances at Court). For several years now, that is since I have taken the demands of my profession as an artist seriously, I can no longer count on any supplementary income from music publishers. My symphonic poems do not bring me a sou in royalties; they even cost me a roundish sum to buy the copies I distribute to a few friends. My Mass, my 'Faust' Symphony etc. are also quite unproductive; and for some years to come I have no expectation of saving any money. . . . If my situation improves, which is not absolutely impossible, I shall take pleasure in alleviating yours.'

There was relatively little travelling during the course of this year, the most important journey being one in August to Budapest, to conduct the first performance of the 'Gran' Mass on the occasion of the consecration of the cathedral. As a native of the country, the composer himself had a royal welcome. But the work suffered some sharp criticism on account of the novelty and boldness of its harmonic language. Nevertheless the clergy declared themselves satisfied. The Cardinal invited Liszt to supper with sixty prelates, proposing his health and making a fine speech to him in Latin. Liszt thereafter paid a brief visit to the Franciscan Monastery of Pest, where he was admitted to the third Order of Saint Francis.

In the same year he completed his Psalm CXXXVII and his 'Dante' Symphony, which was to be dedicated to Richard Wagner. He composed the Beatitudes which were to become the second part of the *Christus* and, after a meeting with the painter Kaulbach on his passage through Munich, he began his *Hunnenschlacht*, a symphonic poem inspired by one of the great canvases of this then much-esteemed artist.

1857   After spending the New Year in bed with a bad attack of furunculosis, Liszt left on a journey through Germany to conduct some of his work, notably the 'Gran' Mass, *Les Préludes* and *Mazeppa*. As many of these were, as usual, charity concerts, for the benefit of certain artists' organisations, they were not very profitable to Liszt.

On the way to Stuttgart, he stopped off for a while to visit that marvellous inspirer of Théophile Gautier, Heine and Chopin: Marie de Kalergis, to whose charms he fell a willing prey. In the company of the 'fairy' whom Gautier celebrated in his *Symphonie en blanc majeur*, he found a little of that gentleness and femininity which his dark and virile Princess almost completely lacked. Liszt had begun to notice this lack particularly over recent months. Carolyne had seemed to want to isolate him from the world and shut him up in the Olympus of Weimar, just at the moment when he was feeling precisely the opposite need, the need for liberty, variety and new horizons. Indeed, in the previous year one of his young pupils, a charming girl called Agnes, had received from him some rather abandoned confidences:

'Your letters are very sweet and very dear to me and it is a good action on your part to think of me, for I am mortally sad and tired ...

I have always the same things to say to you, by the same silences. My heart is constantly bruised and consumed with some sort of prolonged expectation. . . . Thank you for your tenderness and goodness, and for all that grace and simplicity and innate poetry which captivates me . . . '

Liszt suddenly realised that he had need of feminine women. In the lofty intellectual atmosphere, in the rarified air in which Carolyne was trying to confine him, he was beginning to suffocate. With Agnes, and with Marie de Kalergis, he felt a beguiling relaxation. At the same time, on Carolyne's part, he sensed a secret, mounting jealousy.

But he had to go and see his friend. So he left for Zurich to take the score of the 'Dante' Symphony to Wagner, to whom it was dedicated. Wagner was decidedly enthusiastic, to judge by the letter Liszt wrote to him after they had met:

'The important thing is that you should love me and consider my conscientious artistic effort worthy of your regard . . . I confess to you freely that when I brought my composition to you in Zurich, I did not know how you would receive it or what you would think of it. I have already had to hear and read so much about it that in truth I have no opinion at all concerning what I have done. . . . Several quite intimate friends, Joachim for instance, and before that Schumann and others, were so reserved, so vague, almost hostile about my musical output. I do not hold this against them in the least, and cannot do the same for them because their work has never ceased to inspire in me an interest as lively as it is sincere. So you can imagine, my dear Richard, the unspeakable joy it was for me to spend those hours together at Zurich and St. Gallen, when your shining face filled my soul with prolific light, reconciled it to itself and wrapped it around, so to say, with caresses!'

It was during this year that both Liszt's two daughters fell in love. On 18 August, in Berlin, Cosima married Hans von Bülow, the teacher who had taken such pleasure in instructing her. Liszt was present at the wedding. Meanwhile, Blandine had become engaged in Paris to the lawyer Emile Ollivier, whom she was to marry in Florence on 22 October in the presence of Marie d'Agoult.

Hans von Bülow by Frédéric Preller.

At the beginning of September, Weimar was celebrating the centenary of Prince Charles Augustus. There was a crush of royalty as well as painters, musicians and poets from all the German-speaking countries. It was on this occasion that Liszt conducted two very important first performances: the 'Faust' Symphony (recently supplemented by a final Chorus) and *Die Ideale,* from Schiller. The latter fell rather flat, but the first work galvanised the audience. It is in fact the finest of Liszt's symphonic poems.

Just about this time Liszt's Weimar star began to wane. During the September celebrations, certain members of society had cold-shouldered the irregular ménage and Liszt, profoundly hurt, for Carolyne as well as for himself, retired ostentatiously to the Altenburg, shut himself up there and refused to see anyone except those concerned

63

with music. Even among the administrators of the theatre, an undercurrent of intrigue was working against him.

The whole of the latter part of the year was spent travelling in Germany, conducting his works ... and also a little to escape the weight of Carolyne's presence. The Princess was now embarking on her extraordinary career of moraliser. She launched her first draft of *Buddhism and Christianity*, the first volume of the *Ouvrages-fleuves* which she was to go on producing ceaselessly to the end of her life, rather like Marie d'Agoult. Liszt's companions all took to writing, once the grand passion was over, and this one was to do so to a prodigious extent. The year ended on a sad note. It was the end of another cycle for Liszt.

1858   A depressing year. Things did not go well at Weimar, nor in Rome. Liszt was somewhat irritated by the Princess's new state of mind. But it was to her that he dedicated his symphonic poems, in the following terms: 'To her who has fulfilled her faith through love, heightened her hopes through sorrow, built her happiness by sacrifice. To her who remains the companion of my life, the firmament of my

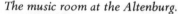

The music room at the Altenburg.

Weimar in 1850.

thought, the living prayer and heaven of my soul. To Jeanne Elisabeth Carolyne.'

Liszt worked on. This year he composed a new, and his last, symphonic poem, entitled *Hamlet*, which was intended to serve as an overture to Shakespeare's play. This was also the time when he began to work at *Two Episodes from Lenau's 'Faust'* from which were to emerge his different versions of the 'Mephisto' Waltz. Finally, he launched his first sketches for the oratorio *St. Elisabeth*.

At Weimar, matters were getting worse. Liszt was trying all the time to push the works of Wagner. A new Intendant had been appointed to the theatre and it was he who was leading the plot against Liszt. The plot succeeded. On 18 December Liszt mounted the rostrum to conduct a charming work which he had rehearsed with the care worthy of the friendship he felt for its author, Cornelius: *The Barber of Baghdad*. There was whistling as the curtain fell. Signalling to the orchestra to stand, he himself applauded the author, who was present in the house, and the same evening submitted his resignation to the Grand Duke. 'Truly', he wrote to Wagner, 'I really need to remind myself that I am a disciple of Saint Francis in order to be able to tolerate so many intolerable things!'

1859 However, Liszt did not leave Weimar at once, but remained there for a further few months. The city where he had done so much good began, however, to feel strange to him. The Grand Duke was no longer interested in music and preferred painting and the theatre. The public followed the tastes of the Prince. Liszt himself became detached from the town he had loved so much, and this caused him a great feeling of loneliness and fatigue. The Princess's divorce proved more and more fraught with problems and Weimar society began to turn its back on the couple who were so persistent in their irregularity. It was to young Agnes that he confided his sorrows, his doubts and the tiredness of his forty-eighth year:

'In the dozen years I have stayed at Weimar, I have been sustained by a feeling not lacking in nobility — the honour, the dignity, the great character of a woman to be protected against infamous persecution — and a great idea: the rebirth of music by its intimate alliance with poetry; a freer and, so to speak, a more appropriate development to the spirit of our times, has always kept me going. This idea, despite the opposition it has encountered and the obstacles put in its way on all sides, has nevertheless made a few strides. No matter what happens, it will triumph unconquerably, for it is an integral part of the sum of the right and true conceptions of our time, and it is a consolation to me to have served it loyally, conscientiously and disinterestedly. Had I wished, during my appointment here in 1848, to rejoin forces with the "posthumous" party in music, to associate myself with its hypocrisies and embrace its prejudices etc., nothing would have been easier for me on account of my former connections with the principal big-wigs in this sphere. I should certainly have gained by it to outward appearances, and in material advantage . . . but this was not to be my lot; my conviction was too sincere, my faith in the present and future of art too intense and too positive to enable me to adjust to these vain, quarrelsome formulae of our pseudo-classicists, who busy themselves crying out that art is dead, is dead . . . '

The correspondence with Wagner continued with the same ardour. But a cloud was to pass over this extraordinary friendship. As Liszt was unable to secure a production of *Rienzi* at Weimar, and as Wagner had run out of resources, the latter wrote to Liszt a short unhappily worded note. Liszt wrote back, referring to two of his own works: 'As the Symphony and the Mass cannot replace good money in the bank, it is useless for me to send them to you. Your urgent telegrams and your wounding letters will from now on be no less superfluous.' But the cloud was quick to pass. Shortly afterwards, Wagner wrote: 'In your hurt, I saw my own unworthiness.' And in October, as Liszt was spending his birthday alone at the Altenburg (Carolyne being in Paris), he received this handsome letter: 'Taking a serious look at our past and present relations,' wrote Wagner, 'I am struck by the solemnity of this day, which must certainly be regarded as one of the most fortunate that Nature can number. Indeed, on this day she gave the world an inestimable treasure . . . .'

And, whilst he was alone, Liszt went on working. He polished up a version of the 'Mephisto' Waltz, finished a new Psalm and began his *Missa Choralis*.

The end of the year brought him a great deal of unhappiness. The day after Christmas, he had an urgent message from Cosima and Bülow that his son Daniel, who was spending a holiday with them in Berlin, and was now twenty years of age, had become seriously ill. The young man, who had been studying law in Vienna, suffered from a chest weakness. Liszt hurried to him immediately, but Daniel died in his father's arms four days later.

FR. EUGENIUS KOPPÁN,

ORDINIS MINORUM S. P. FRANCISCI REFORMATORUM PROVINCIAE HUNGARIAE S. MARIAE MINISTER PROVINCIALIS, ET IN DOMINO SERVUS!

MAGNIFICO, SPECTABILI AC CLARISSIMO

DOMINO DOCTORI

FRANCISCO LISZT,

DOCTORI MUSICES, PLURIUM ORDINUM EQUITI, ARCHI-DUCATUS VAIMARIENSIS SUPREMO AULICAE MUSICES DIRECTORI, SALUTEM ET OMNIGENAM COELESTIUM GRATIARUM AFFLUENTIAM!

Communionem Sanctorum in infinitis Christi meritis radicatam, Sancta Mater Ecclesia pro infinito pariter accepit, retinetque thesauro, adeo, ut ex eodem vivis aeque, ac defunctis tantum, quantum, quibusve ipsa vellet, et illi indigerent, inexhauribiliter dispensandi, et infallibiliter concedendi habeat potestatem. Quod communicationis privilegium, quia speciali authoritate Apostolica ad Superiores Religiosorum Ordinum benigne extensum, concessumque iis esset ideo, ut quidquid ipsi, ac eorum subditi ex meritoriis operibus coram Deo meriti haberent, amicos etiam Ordini suo singulari affectu, et beneficentia propensos, in partem eorumdem meritorum speciali privilegio communicationis vocare, et efficaciter recipere possint: idcirco ubi Praetitulatam Magnificentiam Vestram singulari erga Ordinem nostrum affectus et beneficentiae propensione devotam esse comperio, pro temporali spiritualem mercedem gratitudine religiosa compensando, praefatam Magnificentiam Vestram Speciali Vinculo in Confraternitatem Provinciae Nostrae Marianae sincere recipio, ac assumo, ita quidem, ut in omnibus meritis Fratrum curae meae concreditorum, immo et successorum nostrorum speciali communicatione in vita, et post mortem particeps esse valeat. Divinam subinde super hoc enixe precor clementiam, ut haec specialis Communio Sanctorum in coelo, et in terra rata, et confirmata maneat, in nomine Patris, et Filii, et Spiritus Sancti. Amen.

Dabam in Conventu nostro Posoniensi die 23. Junii 1857.

Fr. Eugenius Koppán,
Minister Provincialis.

> Yes, the crucified Jesus, the Passion of the
> Exaltation of the Holy Cross, this was my true vocation!
> *Franz*

> Your soul is too tender, too artistic, too full
> of feeling to remain without feminine society.
> *Carolyne*

THE FRANCISCAN

At the beginning of 1860 came great news: it was learned that the Princess's divorce had been pronounced. But, through some intrigue or other, the Bishop of Fulda did not accept the decision as valid. Carolyne decided to go to Rome immediately and intervene personally. She left Weimar in May and Liszt, dejected and tired, stayed on at the Altenburg. He did work a little, however, despite his misfortunes. His first preoccupation was a complete edition of his songs, but he also continued with his composition of *St. Elisabeth,* though without much enthusiasm. Once again, Agnes was to be the recipient of his confidences:

'In certain rarely frequented regions of art, there is a sort of Jacob's

ificate of Ordination as a member of the
ıciscan Order, June 1857

struggle between thought and style, feeling and technique. . . . Work is given to us both as a penalty and as a liberation . . . I am mortally sad and can say nothing, hear nothing. Only prayer can give me relief at times, but, alas! I can no longer pray for long at a time, however imperious the need I feel. May God help me to overcome this moral crisis and may His mercy lighten my darkness.'

It was now, not unnaturally, that he made his will, a document which deserves quotation:

'This is my Will. It is made on this 14th day of September 1860, when the Church celebrates the Exaltation of the Holy Cross. The name of this festival also expresses the burning and mysterious feeling which has marked my whole life as with a sacred stigma. Yes, the crucified Jesus, the Passion of the Exaltation of the Holy Cross, this was my true vocation. I have felt it deep in my heart from the age of seventeen, when I asked with prayers and supplications to be admitted to the Paris Seminary, hoping that it would be granted me to live the life of the saints and perhaps to die the death of martyrs. It was not so, alas! But not once since then, despite all the sins and errors I have committed and for which I feel a sincere repentance and contrition, has the divine light of the Cross been entirely withdrawn from me. At times it has even flooded my spirit with its glory. I give thanks to God, and shall die with my soul abandoned to the Cross, our redemption and supreme blessing. And to bear witness to my faith, I wish to receive the holy sacrament of the Apostolic and Roman Catholic Church before my death, thus obtaining the remission and absolution of my sins, Amen.

'Whatever good I may have done and thought over the past twelve years I owe to Her I have so fervently wished to call my wife – a wish obstinately opposed by human malice and the most deplorable caprices of the law – to Jeanne Elisabeth Carolyne, Princess Wittgenstein, née Iwanowska. I cannot write her name without an ineffable tremor. All my joy has come from her, and all my suffering turns to her for appeasement. Not only has she associated herself and identified herself completely with my existence, my work, my worries, my career – helping me with her advice, sustaining me by her encouragement, reviving me with her enthusiasm in an unimaginable prodigality of care, forethought, wise and gentle words, ingenious and persistent effort. But more than that, she has often sacrificed herself, abdicating from that which is legitimately imperative in her nature, in order to be better able to shoulder my burden, which she has transformed into her riches and her only luxury . . . .

'I should have liked to possess an immense genius to sing this sublime soul in sublime harmonies. Alas! I have scarcely succeeded in stammering out a few thin notes which are gone with the wind. If, however, something of my musical labours were to remain (and I have applied myself to them with overwhelming fervour for ten years) let it be those pages in which Carolyne has most part by the inspiration of her heart.

'I beg her to pardon me for the sad insufficiency of my work as an artist, as well as that, still more painful, of my good intentions, enmeshed as they were in so many failings and incongruities. She knows that the most poignant grief of my life is not to have felt sufficiently worthy of her and not to have been able to raise and hold myself to that pure and holy region where her spirit and her virtue reside.'

Then follow some financial arrangements, and he goes on:

'There is in contemporary art a glorious name, which will increase in glory: Richard Wagner. His genius has been a torch to me, and I have followed it. My friendship for Wagner has preserved all the characteristics of a noble passion. At one time (about twelve years ago now) I dreamed of a new era for Weimar, comparable to that of Charles Augustus, of which Wagner and I should be the leading lights, as Goethe and Schiller once were. The shabbiness, not to say the villainy, of certain local circumstances, all sorts of jealousies and ineptitudes here and elsewhere, have prevented the realisation of this dream, which was to be to the honour of the present Grand Duke. Notwithstanding all this, I am still of the same sentiment and conviction, which it was only too easy to make clear to everyone. And I urge Carolyne to agree to continue our affectionate relationship with Wagner after my death. Who better than she could understand the high purpose given to art by Wagner, his divine feeling for love and poetry?'

Then came further detailed arrangements. No-one is forgotten.

'Finally I ask Carolyne again to send on my behalf to Madame Caroline d'Artigaux, née Comtesse de Saint-Cricq (at Pau) one of my talismans mounted in a ring.' He concludes: 'Upon this, I kneel once more with Carolyne to pray, as we have often done together. I wish to be buried simply, without any ceremony and, if possible, at night.'

1861 He had poured out his heart, but appeasement did not follow. He remained depressed and defeated in his solitude at the Altenburg. This depression became almost a sickness. 'My entire life', he wrote, 'is nothing but a long Odyssey of feeling and love. I was fit only for love and hitherto, alas, I have only loved badly!'

During his joyless labours, one family incident brought some sweetness. He went to Berlin to the christening of his first granddaughter, Cosima's daughter, Daniela-Senta.

Carolyne, meanwhile, was agitating in Rome, apparently still without success.

In the spring Liszt made a trip to Paris. There he put up a show of leading a worldly existence, visiting Blandine and Ollivier and meeting poor Berlioz and the aged Rossini. He went to see Marie, whom he had not seen for sixteen years, and conversed aimlessly with her on political matters. Wagner was also in Paris and introduced Liszt to Baudelaire. There was a good deal of fêting and Napoleon III presented Liszt with the order of Commander of the Légion d'Honneur.

Then he came back to spend the summer in Weimar where he conducted his last festival, the Festival of Composers, which, thanks to his efforts, was to enjoy a more resounding success than usual that year. The whole musical world was present. Wagner himself attended and was at the theatre for a rehearsal of the 'Faust' Symphony, conducted by Bülow. He was carrying under his arm an enormous tome – the completed score of *Tristan*.

The Festival was hardly over when Liszt had an urgent message from the Princess: all was arranged; the marriage was fixed for 22 October, 'Saint Liszt's day' – his fiftieth birthday. Liszt set off on 17 August. Before leaving, he announced his imminent arrival in Rome to Carolyne. 'It is impossible to contain under one roof the emotions of my last hours at the Altenburg. Every room, every piece of furniture, down to the steps of the staircase and the lawn in the garden, everything was lit with your love, without which I felt as though annihilated . . . I could not hold back my tears. But after another few moments at your *prie-dieu,* where you used to kneel with me before I embarked on any journey, I felt a sort of liberation which comforted me . . . . Leaving this house, I feel nearer to you and I can breathe more freely.'

After a visit to the Prince of Hohenzollern at Löwenberg, Liszt passed through Marseille on 14 October and arrived in Rome on 20th. He was in no great hurry, apparently!

On the evening of the 21st, Franz and Carolyne took communion and kept a holy vigil together in the Princess's house on the Piazza di Spagna. The wedding, fixed for the next day, threw Roman society into a turmoil. Suddenly, in the night, there was a knocking at the door of the Princess's apartment. A priest had brought a message from the Vatican. The Pope was asking to see the documents again, for it had been brought to his attention that the reasons for divorce were open to question. This, needless to say, was the result of the renewed intrigues of the Prince of Wittgenstein. Yet again, the marriage was frustrated.

1862 After this new reverse, Liszt remained in Rome, installing himself in a very modest apartment at 113 Via Felice. He visited Carolyne every day, but as time went by this gradually became something of an unwelcome obligation. The Princess was enveloped from morning to night in the smoke of her cigars, editing her enormous religious, philosophical and political treatises. As a matter of interest, here are some of the titles: *Buddhism and Christianity* (one volume); *Matter in Christian Dogma* (three volumes); *Practical Homilies for Society Women* (one volume); *Religion and Morality* (one volume); *Short Practical Homilies for the use of Society Women during Spiritual Retreat* (eight volumes); *Simplicity of Doves, Wisdom of Serpents: some Reflections suggested by today's Women and Times* (one volume); *Suffering and Wisdom* (one volume); *On Christian Perfection and the Inner Life* (one volume); *Internal Causes of the External Weakness of the Church* (twenty-four volumes). It is conceivable that Liszt, saintly though he was, did not find life here very amusing. A curious thing was

73

that, as has often been remarked, the faith that had joined these two together was in some degree responsible for parting them. The serious, blue-stocking religiosity of the Princess began to bore the romantic Christian in Liszt. Moreover, at the Princess's establishment he was the object of a sort of ostentatious cult. Carolyne's salon was strewn with fourteen busts representing Liszt at all ages. All this irritated him. Nevertheless he immersed himself in work.

1863 *St. Elisabeth* was the first work Liszt tackled. He was still to some extent taken up with worldly life as well. The Princess's salon was in a sense worldly, frequented by the Duc de Sermoneta, Laura Monghetti, Tarnowsky, Bache, Sgambati, Cardinal Lucien Bonaparte, Monsignor Lichnowsky and Monsignor Hohenlohe. But no sooner had he lifted himself out of his former depression than he wanted to get away from this circle. Escape was made easier from him by the news of a fresh bereavement: his daughter Blandine had just died in Saint Tropez, where she had given birth to a son, Daniel. From then on, he led a very retired life, going less and less frequently to see the Princess, to whom, however, he wrote long and edifying letters.

To complete his isolation, he left the Via Felice and went to live a hermit's life on the Monte Mario in the cloister of the Madonna del Rosario, where the archivist of the Vatican lived. It was there that Pope Pius IX came to visit him. Liszt played the harmonium and treated him to his ideas on the reform of religious music; and Pius IX invited him to a Mass which he himself said.

However, his spirit of retreat was not so exclusive that he did not agree to accept the invitation of Bülow to the Karlsruhe Festival. There his works were performed and met with success. On his return, he passed through Munich, where he met Wagner and was taken to the latter's house at the Starnbergersee.

1864 From then on, he was to take a number of jaunts outside Rome. That year, he went back to Weimar, a town now dead to art (a cause of great sadness to Liszt) and then to Berlin to see his daughter Cosima. They left together for Paris, where he was to stay for quite a while with the Olliviers and where he was also able to visit his aged mother.

In Rome, he did less work than usual. *St. Elisabeth* was now finished. But he did add a few sheets to his *Années de pèlerinage:* that was to be the third book.

Nevertheless there was to be an important event this year, otherwise so apparently uneventful: the death of Prince Wittgenstein. Was the marriage of Franz and Carolyne, thus made possible, now to take place? To everyone's amazement, there was no longer any question of this. The confirmation of this unexpected decision was not slow to follow in the ensuing months.

1865   On 25 April, in fact, Liszt took minor Orders. He was without doubt prepared for this step, but it was also thought that he hastened it in order to escape a marriage which no longer interested him. Needless to say, the Princess took a different view all along. The Pope's interdict of 1861 had apparently come as a providential warning to her.

Liszt's ordination naturally made European news and unleashed as many jokes as the famous sword of honour at Budapest had done earlier. 'Liszt has composed Masses in order to accustom himself to saying them,' exclaimed Rossini. Marie d'Agoult riddled him with sarcasm, and the following reply was attributed to Liszt in answer to someone who questioned him about the celibacy of priests: 'Gregory VII was a great philanthropist.' There was talk of fittings for soutanes which had taken place before ordination at the house of Monsignor Hohenlohe and, in fact, there was every kind of rumour about this event which Liszt had wanted to be so simple and which, unknown to him, was to become a most spectacular affair. He had always tended to be unconscious of such things, so it was not without reason that Jean Chantavoine made an amusing comparison, worth repeating, on the subject of his taking Orders:

'At the end of a concert he had given in Prague in 1840, as the enthusiasm of his audience demanded an encore, for which they wanted him to play his *Ave Maria* (after Schubert), Liszt first played the *Hexameron.* On further insistence, still rebellious, he embarked, not on

75

the *Ave Maria* but on one of the most vertiginous of his bravura pieces: the *Galop chromatique* and, by a transition as unexpected as it was elegant, continued with the *Ave Maria*. In one sense Liszt's personality is contained in that transition from the *Galop chromatique* to the *Ave Maria*. When one attempts to recount and explain his life story, one must have a virtuosity as great as his own in order to trace the transition from romantic adventure to Holy Orders. But this is not possible. The attraction of his personality lies precisely in that only he could pass from the *Galop chromatique* to the *Ave Maria* without disrupting the modulations and without playing any false notes.'
It could hardly be better said.

But amongst all this disturbance, Liszt continued to work unperturbed. First, a little theology, for, on the evening of the ceremony, he had been received by the Pope, who had advised him to press on with his studies in this direction. But above all he devoted himself passionately to the composition of his *Christus*. The occupations of the moment still reflected the same paradoxes, for while administering Mass with devotion and reading his breviary conscientiously, he never forgot

*The Abbé Liszt in Rome
(silhouette by Schulze).*

he was a virtuoso. In May 1865, some days after his ordination, he wrote to the Princess: 'My day here is spent reading about fifty pages of the Catechism of Perseverance in Italian and in searching on the piano for some ideas as to how to deal with the Indian jugglery of *l'Africaine*.'

It was at this time that he moved house once again and went to live at the Vatican.

On 15 August he went to Budapest to conduct the first performance of *St. Elisabeth* and then the 'Dante' Symphony, which was triumphantly received. During the course of a concert, he sat down at the piano in public for the first time for a very long while and he played two *Légendes* of the two Saints Francis. One evening, a crowd collected under his window to salute him: for these eight or ten thousand people, the Abbé Liszt had a piano pushed out on to the balcony and played some Hungarian Rhapsodies.

1866   The winter in Rome was calm. In his retreat, Liszt worked at his *Christus*. In early spring he learned of the death of his mother, a few days before leaving for Paris to conduct the 'Gran' Mass and some of his symphonic poems. The journey to France was for him a mixture of glorifications and disappointments. He was officially received with the greatest of honour, but on the musical plane some wounding experiences were awaiting him. Certainly, Camille Saint-Saëns and the great pianist Francis Planté gave him an enthusiastic welcome. But after the performance of the Mass at Saint Eustache — conducted by Liszt himself — the press was more than tepid. The occasion drew a vast audience and the takings were among the largest of the period. But it had no real repercussions. The 'happy few' create the law. And the happy few preferred the much vaunted pianist of earlier times to the newly ordained Abbé. Musical circles were particularly ferocious and gave evidence of a lack of understanding which was disturbing to the great and daring innovator in the field of language as in that of aesthetics. Berlioz left after the performance declaring: 'This Mass is the negation of art' and d'Ortigue made a pun which was perhaps no worse than any other but which was clearly not worthy of the occasion: *'Eloignez de moi ce caliszt' (calice)*. These sarcasms did not fail to reach Marie d'Agoult through an article in *La Liberté*, to which she claimed to contribute music criticism. It is understandable that Liszt did not want to see her. However, one day, his son-in-law Ollivier managed to entice him to her house — it was apparently she who had wanted this, but the conversation lagged and everyone was embarrassed. Marie showed herself up as pretentious and Liszt in his irritation threw in her face the unworthiness of her shabby book *Nélida*. There the matter rested.

So the net result of his trip was negative. Berlioz's bad temper, particularly, pained him, after what he, Liszt, had done for him at Weimar. The impressions he sent to Carolyne are summed up rather well in this single sentence: 'Success, yes — sensation even — but a difficult situation. Saint Gregory will help us.' That 'Saint Gregory will help us' says much to express his disappointment.

Back in Rome, Liszt got to work again, finished his *Christus* and composed a Mass commissioned for the coronation of the Emperor Franz Joseph in Hungary. Then, during the summer and early autumn, when Rome had once more begun to tire him rather, there were more travels. First to Budapest for the coronation celebrations, where he was to conduct; then to Weimar for the 800th anniversary of the Wartburg; and finally to Munich where he conducted the *St. Elisabeth* and heard *Tannhäuser* and *Lohengrin*.

It was also in Munich that he met Bülow, newly appointed Director of the Conservatoire and in charge of the main operatic events. The Cosima-Wagner drama, which had been hatching for five years, was now well into its second act. It had all begun in the summer five years before. Cosima was taking a cure at the Reichenhall watering place at the time, in Upper Bavaria. After the Weimar Festival where, as we have seen, Liszt had conducted for the last time and at which Wagner had been present, the two men, accompanied by Blandine and Emile Ollivier, spent a few days with Cosima. The beauty of this female incarnation of Liszt made a violent impression on Wagner. Cosima, who had been married to Bülow for nine years, was then in the full bloom of her thirtieth year. A quarter of a century separated the two, who were to be united by a single look. But not a word had been said, either then or during their various encounters in Frankfurt in 1862 and again in 1863 at the Gewandhaus in Leipzig, where Bülow was playing Liszt's

Concerto in E flat. It was not until 28 November 1864 that Richard and Cosima declared their hitherto silently pledged love: Wagner was on his way to Berlin and it was during a carriage drive that they spoke to each other and decided to make the secret known. Bülow had been the intimate friend and defender of Wagner for about twenty years. The huge volume of letters addressed by the composer to his interpreter bears witness to a very deep and solid mutual affection. From that fatal day in November 1864, the name of Cosima completely disappeared from the letters which Wagner continued to write to Bülow. For two such complete persons as Wagner and Cosima, nothing could halt the march of destiny and Bülow was gradually brought up against the facts. From being perhaps genuinely ignorant of them, he was forced into the position of wishing to be so. This attitude hardened in the following two years, and he could find refuge from his grief only in frenetic work.

Liszt already saw that the only thing to do was to assure Bülow of his affection. He knew his own daughter too well. And so he left Munich again for Rome.

1867   There were no particularly important events in this year. Liszt led a reclusive life, going to Munich from time to time to advise and help Bülow, both with his administration of the Conservatoire and with his own personal tragedy. In October, Liszt took a great decision: he would go to see Wagner in Triebschen and try to persuade him to give up the relationship. He arrived at Lucerne on the 9th. Wagner, aging but still exuberant and passionate, was waiting and eager to see him. Here, no doubt, lay the charm which explains why during the brief visit Liszt seems not to have touched on the unhappy subject which had brought him there. It should also be said that Wagner had played the recently completed third act of the *Meistersinger* on the piano for Liszt. The beauty of it drove everything from Liszt's memory for the moment. And when he went back to Munich to see Bülow, he told him enigmatically: 'I have seen Napoleon at Saint Helena.'

Being of a wandering disposition, Liszt did not go straight back to Rome on his return to Italy, but lingered long and fervently in the holy places. Assisi, Notre Dame de Lorette, Grotta Mare.

With Cosima, 1867.

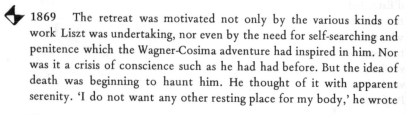

1868 A reclusive year in Rome, one of the rare uneventful years in the history of Liszt's career.

1869 The retreat was motivated not only by the various kinds of work Liszt was undertaking, nor even by the need for self-searching and penitence which the Wagner-Cosima adventure had inspired in him. Nor was it a crisis of conscience such as he had had before. But the idea of death was beginning to haunt him. He thought of it with apparent serenity. 'I do not want any other resting place for my body,' he wrote to Carolyne, 'but the cemetery near where I die, nor do I want any religious ceremony other than a low mass (without any sung Requiem) in the parish.' This serenity is astonishing in one of Liszt's nature. But it will be seen that although all this was perfectly sincere, the composer of the Rhapsodies was still eager to live.

At the beginning of the year he was called to Weimar, where the Grand Duke wished to see him and expressed the desire for his permanent presence. A charming house, fully appointed by the Duke, was offered to Liszt. This was the Hofgärtnerei, one-time residence of the Court's head gardener. Liszt accepted the offer and, when he came back, was fêted in just the same way as he had been before. He was surrounded by beautiful women and ravishing pupils. 'They all love themselves in me,' he observed amiably. Then followed a delirium of music, courses, lessons in piano and chamber music. Passionately, and with a quite new and high-spirited youthfulness, he applied himself to the piano, giving interpretation courses which left unforgettable memories in the minds of those who were privileged to attend them.

Friends flocked in from all parts. The second Weimar reign was beginning. All this was not without its irritations for the Princess, who continued to turn out her gigantic works in Roman solitude. But perhaps she sensed that the only way of keeping this exceptional creature was to leave him a certain degree of liberty. She was however, to prove less tolerant when, during the course of a longer visit from Liszt in the autumn, she was to discover his involvement with a passionate pupil, the Comtesse Janina, who fell madly in love with him and demonstrated it with all the turbulence of her Cossack origins. To say that Liszt was unmoved by these excesses would no doubt be short of the truth. He defended himself honestly, sublimely, by prayer. He even fled and took refuge with the cardinal of Hohenlohe at the Villa d'Este, believing that there he would find shelter from any invasion. But one day there came a ravishing young man with armfuls of flowers who threw himself at Liszt's feet. It was Janina in disguise. It is difficult to know what happened after that, but why should we not accept the version, so Liszt-like in its poetry, offered by Guy de Pourtalès: 'Liszt worked at his *Beethoven Festkantate* and kept by him the *Christian Perfection* recently written by Carolyne. This time, however, the

Olga Janina

handsome gardener of love prevailed over all talismans.'

The year 1869 brought another emotional disturbance for Liszt. This was the final break between Wagner and Bülow. Cosima's fate was decided. The last lines of the last letter addressed by the composer to his faithful and ardent interpreter were 'We are both sufficiently unhappy not to delude ourselves any longer about anything, for there is no longer anything we can do to help each other.' For a long time now Liszt had had no illusions on the subject.

 1870   A year of renewed activity. Liszt settled himself early on in the Hofgärtnerei in Weimar and prepared for the Festival he was to direct, at the request of the Grand Duke, at the beginning of the following summer. Then he went to Budapest to lay the foundations of future activity: the Directorship and Presidency of the Royal Academy of Music. After various journeys to Germany and Austria, he came back to Weimar for the Festival, which was due to run from 15 June until 6 July, and of which he was the great master of ceremonies. Here he conducted the *Beethoven Festkantate* which he had been composing at the Villa d'Este when Janina broke in. The programmes of the Music Festival were a triumph for Wagner, with performances of *Tannhäuser*, *Lohengrin, The Flying Dutchman* and the *Meistersinger,* but they were also triumphs of Liszt's will, friendship and tenacity. This apotheosis took place, by an irony of fate, some weeks before the event which was to mark the break between Liszt and Wagner: the marriage of Cosima and Wagner on 25 August. Liszt also broke with his daughter.

Meanwhile, the success of the Weimar Festival was complete — a marvellous revenge for Liszt. The reign of 'Saint Liszt' had really begun. The whole of European society was assembled there: kings, princes, artists, pupils. Marie de Moukhanoff-Kalergis wrote:

'All unfriendliness is silenced in the presence of the great Liszt, who has never appeared better or greater . . . . He brought his infinite grace to every detail, his sensitive regard for each and all, friendly to the smallest, distributing praise and advice, on his feet from seven in the morning, playing, conducting, talking all day, and all this as he is approaching sixty. He gives strength to all around him and his own is not diminished . . . . One becomes drunk with music and ideals in a warmth of enthusiasm, a unanimity of admiration, which are encountered nowhere else.'

As soon as the triumphant Festival was over, Liszt left immediately for Munich, where the first performance of the *Valkyrie* was given on 26 June. Wagner was not present.

The Franco-Prussian war had torn Liszt, the passionate cosmopolitan, apart, and he took shelter for a while with a Hungarian friend. From there, he wrote to Carolyne:

'After the terrifying blow of the surrender of the French Army and

83

of the Emperor, I shall have to give up for some considerable time the hopes held out to me in your letter. Providence has pronounced her decree against the sovereign whom I admired as the cleverest and best figure of our time . . . . No doubt some great idea will emerge from the catastrophe and we shall see some principle of the modern state appear. But the philosophy of history is a very conjectural science even today, bound round with fear . . . . Politics is the science of opportunity and the art of the relevant. Obviously, Mr. Bismarck understands this better than anyone at this present time! I do not have to follow him into these lofty regions, and shall occupy myself wholeheartedly with "Saint Stanislaus". Let us pray that the Kingdom of God will come.'

And he did in fact set to work on his *Saint Stanislaus,* based on one of the Princess's texts, and devoted himself to it for the whole of the rest of the year.

In Rome, the two old lovers continued not to see each other very often. Carolyne remained immersed in her apologetics. Liszt avoided visiting her, knowing that she was a great talker and that discussion, on however high a plane of thought, might arise at any moment. He preferred to write to her at leisure and at length on all sorts of edifying subjects.

Moreover, was not liberty the most precious of possessions? Liszt thought so, but not the Princess. She, seeing him ceaselessly attracted towards Weimar and Budapest, tried to supply a mentor for him in the person of Mademoiselle Adelheit von Schorn, at least for the duration of his visits to Weimar.

1871   At the beginning of the year, according to his now established custom, Liszt installed himself at Weimar. The 'guardian angel' supplied for him by Carolyne soon exasperated him by the indiscretion of the reports she sent to Rome.

Once the Weimar season was over, Liszt returned to Rome, delighted to escape the watchful eye of Mademoiselle Adelheit von Schorn. Just as he was about to settle down quietly to work, he was bombarded with letters from his old Cossack flame, the Countess Janina, joyously announcing her impending arrival from New York. Liszt replied rather rudely, and left eagerly for Budapest, where the new Academy of Music required his services. Janina had meanwhile received his letter, politely but firmly rebuffing her. Before setting off by the shortest possible route, she telegraphed him: 'Am leaving this week in reply to your letter'. From Rome, where she arrived too late, she left for Budapest, where she disembarked in full fury, laden not with flowers but with a belt-full of pistols. In the end, her plan to kill Liszt merely gave her a nervous breakdown, and the overwrought young woman was shipped back to Paris where she was to write in revenge two volcanic but quite uninteresting tracts: *Souvenirs of a Cossack* and *Souvenirs of a Pianist*.

But Liszt was used to women who wrote too much. From Budapest, he came back to Rome, where the Princess received him severely, not because of the outrageous Janina incident, about which, needless to say, all Europe was talking, but because she had learned, rather belatedly, of the ineffectiveness of the 'guardian angel' at Weimar. During his last visit, Liszt had been carried away by the company of a very pretty lady, the Baroness of Meyendorff, who was as austere as she was passionate and who had recently been widowed. Again the storm passed quickly. Moreover, it appears to have been the last. Carolyne was never again to have cause to frown.

1872　　From now on, Liszt observed a certain regularity in his activities, balanced between the two habitual visits to Weimar and Budapest.

On 22 May, Wagner's birthday, the foundation stone of the Bayreuth theatre was laid. The two men had neither seen nor written to each other for a long time. Liszt had obviously no intention of attending, not having been invited. However, forty-eight hours before the event, he received the following letter from Wagner, dated 18 May:

'My dear and great friend,

Cosima maintains that you will not come, even though I invite you. Must we still bear this pain; we who have already borne so much? But not to invite you would be impossible for me. What appeal shall I then add to the word: "come"? You came into my life as the greatest man I was ever able to call friend, and then slowly detached yourself from me, perhaps because the affection you bore me was never so great as mine for you . . . . But someone has taken your place, increasing my nostalgic desire to feel you near me: it is your truest, profoundest being which has been reborn and come to me. You are thus living in all your beauty before my eyes and in my heart, and we are joined as though beyond the grave. You were the first whose love ennobled me. Joined with this love in a second, higher life, I am now capable of things I should never have found possible alone. So you have become everything for me, whilst I have remained of so little significance to you. You see how much the better share I have! To say to you, "come" is to say "come to yourself!" For it is yourself you will find here. May God bless and cherish you, whatever you decide.

Your old friend,
Richard'

There is a certain amount of deceit, a passable cleverness and a great deal of the sublime heart-cry in this letter. There was no resisting it. Liszt wrote immediately:

'Dear and admirable friend,

Deeply moved by your letter, I can find no words to thank you. My fervent hope is that the ghost of things which attach me to the past will disappear and that we shall soon be able to see each other again. For you must have dazzling proof that my soul has remained indissolubly attached to *you* – a soul regenerated and ready to participate in your second and higher life, where you are capable of what you could not do before. I shall have Heaven's forgiveness because I say: May the Lord's blessing be upon you, as is all my love.

20 May 1872, Weimar,   F.L.

I cannot bear to send these lines by post. They will come to you on 22 May via a woman who has known for years how I think and feel.'

It was the famous 'guardian angel', Mlle von Schorn, who took the train and brought the letter to Wagner.

Reconciliation was complete. In the letters which were to be exchanged between Liszt and Wagner in the future they were to address each other in such terms as 'my august friend' or 'most sublime', or 'incredible friend', or 'still more incredible friend', etc., but the reconciliation was to be sealed with a prompt reunion. This took place in September, when Liszt went to spend a few days at Bayreuth with the family and the five children. The theatre was already fairly far

The Festspielhaus in Bayreuth

advanced and Wagner showed Liszt his first work on *Parsifal*. Liszt had absolutely forgiven his daughter. 'Others may judge or condemn her,' he said. 'For me she remains a spirit worthy of the great pardon of Saint Francis, and admirably my daughter.'

This good understanding was far from pleasing to Carolyne, however. She had never really liked the Wagners and had always feared for Liszt's cultivation of them.

1873   The Princess showed her feelings to a marked degree and so sourly that Liszt had to get away from her. Almost the whole of the winter of 1872-73 he spent in Budapest, where he was Director of the Academy.

Back in Weimar in the spring, he conducted the first performance of his *Christus,* an oratorio which was greeted as a great success by an enormous international audience.

After this, still against the will of the Princess, he spent the summer at Bayreuth and this period was, according to his own account, to be one of the happiest of his later years.

In September, he devoted three weeks to Carolyne who, still shut up in her scribbler's retreat in Rome, veiled her reproaches. She wrote:

'Your soul is too tender, too artistic, too full of feeling, to remain without feminine society, you need women around you, and women of every sort, just as an orchestra requires different instruments and variety of tone. Unfortunately, there are few women who are as they should be – good and sincere and responsive to your intelligence without laying a blameworthy hand upon chords which, if they sound at all, sound unhappy. I am often sad to think how you will remain misunderstood. Your triumphs may seem in times to come rather like Bacchanalia, because a few Bacchantes joined in them.'

Autumn found Liszt back in Budapest, where there were jubilee celebrations in his honour: the fiftieth anniversary of the first concert he had given in Vienna, when Beethoven had embraced him. After daylong festivities of the sort his countrymen had always treated him to, he gave a few concerts in Vienna, Pressburg and Oedenburg, the scenes of his first exploits.

But all these celebrations exhausted him, and it was with some satisfaction that he returned to Italy and installed himself at the Villa d'Este where he was to spend several happy and peaceful months deep in the composition of *St. Cecilia* and of *Die Glocken des Strassburger Münsters*. Liszt led a regular life, not emerging from his solitude except on Sundays to visit the Princess.

1874 The peaceful Roman life continued and was untroubled this year except by the sad news of the loss of his old friend Maria Moukhanoff. The regret he felt inspired his *Elegy in memory of Countess Maria Moukhanoff, née Countess Nesselrode*.

1875 Travels began again in the spring. At Budapest Wagner and Liszt took turns on the rostrum, the former to conduct fragments from the *Ring* and the latter to play a Beethoven piano concerto. Then came Munich and Hanover, and finally Weimar at the beginning of June. Here, the Grand Duke organised a memorial celebration to the woman who had been his great friend, Maria Moukhanoff. An international assembly of monarchs and artists was brought together for the occasion. In front of a catafalque of flowers and turf on which was mounted the portrait of Maria, Liszt conducted his Requiem, the *Ave Maria,* The *Hymne de l'enfant à son réveil, St. Cecilia* and the *Elegy.* And it was Liszt who pronounced a few words at her funeral oration: 'There was in her some sort of mysterious note which found its harmony only in heaven.'

1876 A glorious year, but one of mourning as well. Glorious because, in August, Liszt witnessed the apotheosis of all the ideas he had always upheld. Before an audience of sovereigns, disciples, tourists, musicians, the Bayreuth theatre was inaugurated (13 August, with the *Rheingold*). Liszt was at the peak of his enthusiasm and happiness and could not restrain himself from telling Carolyne, 'No more doubts or obstacles; the immense genius of Wagner has surmounted them all. His work *The Ring of the Nibelungen* shines on the world. The blind cannot put out its light nor the deaf its music.' The Princess took this explosion of joy rather badly. Wagner's triumph exasperated her, and she wrote Liszt letters full of reproach, accusing him of simply playing the part of stooge. Her hurtful remarks did not affect Liszt who, far from playing such a part, was on the contrary receiving the homage due to his fidelity and friendship. At the great banquet which took place after the Cycle, Wagner rose and, in the presence of eight hundred guests, pointed out Liszt, saying: 'There is the one who first had confidence in me, the man without whom you might never have heard a note of my music, my very dear friend, Franz Liszt.'

And it was a year of mourning because, a little earlier, in June, when Liszt was in Budapest, he had read in the papers of the death of Marie d'Agoult, and a letter from Ronchaud was to give him details: 'Madame d'Agoult's illness was very short, and we did not know how dangerous it was until the day before she died . . . . She died of pneumonia, caught whilst she was out walking. She suffered greatly during the first days; later, things were more peaceful.' Liszt tried to feel some emotion, but without success, it seems, since he wrote later: 'The most desirable of sacraments to receive seems to me to be that of Extreme Unction.'

And in September came the news of George Sand's death.

That winter, Liszt did not return to Rome. The exchange of letters with Carolyne had been somewhat sharp after the reproaches she had made. Alluding to her reference to the rôle of 'stooge', he had replied:

'No one plays parts here. We create and enjoy art . . . . In all humility, I do not believe I deserve the letter I have had from you today . . . God knows that to allay your sufferings has been my sole task for many years. For my part, I wish to remember only those times when we have wept and prayed together as from one heart. After your letter of today, I shall not return to Rome.'

1877   But he did go back, although not until the following summer. In the meantime, he had been all over Europe: Weimar, Budapest and a short stay on the banks of the Rhine where Bülow was resting, worn out with concert tours in which he had been both playing and conducting. Liszt was eager to see him, for his former son-in-law, turning his back on the Wagnerian cause which he had previously so ardently defended, had taken up what was then believed to be the opposite one — that of Brahms. He had said things which his old friends found rather unfortunate, and although there was some excuse for this in human terms, in artistic terms it was nonetheless wrong. The impression Bülow left on Liszt was that: 'His suffering is moral rather than physical. His innate heroism remains, and will, I hope, render him victorious over the double sickness which oppresses him.'

Back then to Rome. Liszt installed himself at Tivoli, where he worked away quietly. For his third book of the *Années de pèlerinage* he composed the two threnodies: *Aux cyprès de la Villa d'Este, Angelus! Prière aux anges* and the *Sursum corda*. He redoubled his religious practices and found a deep happiness and peace in them, directly reflected in these works.

Of course, there were skirmishes with Carolyne from time to time. And these were now no longer of a religious nature, but concerned politics and all the great general questions of life. In this year of 1877, Liszt wrote to the Princess:

'The great grief of my later days is to find myself in disagreement with you. This was not so in the years between 1847 and 1862 ... Rome, and your transcendancy of mind, have changed all that ... . Ever since the Syllabus — to which I conform and submit myself in accordance with Catholic duty — we have constantly been at variance on the subject of Rome, Pest and Weimar.'

True, the phrasing is careful. The expression 'your transcendancy of mind' is not without malice. But the tone is no less firm for that. The 'lazybones' is saying exactly what he thinks to his 'good cleric'.

1878   Every now and again over the years he had been going back to his *Saint Stanislaus,* of which it will be remembered the Princess had written the text. But he had little enthusiasm for it.

He made a few trips to Germany and Hungary, then returned to Paris where, on the occasion of the Universal Exhibition, his 'Gran' Mass was produced at Saint-Eustache by Pasdeloup. He had hesitated before going there, for he had very bad memories of his visit in 1866 when Berlioz and other old friends had behaved so badly towards him.

In any case, he made it clear that he had no wish to appear either as 'an old pianist' or as 'a young composer'. And, referring to his disappointing friends, he wrote to Saint-Saëns:

'I should not like to give up entirely the idea of meeting them again, although the bad performance of the 'Gran' Mass in 1866 and the resultant verbiage left a painful impression on me. This is simply explained on all sides. Nevertheless to expose myself again to such misunderstandings would be too much. Without false modesty or stupid vanity, I could not count myself among the famous pianists who have lost themselves in bad compositions.'

This idea obsessed him, and very legitimately; it was something the Princess had never ceased to repeat to him, to the point of exasperation, in her desire to see him break with certain people she herself found it difficult to tolerate.

Liszt went to Paris all the same. The 'Gran' Mass was an enormous success and took a considerable amount of money for those days: 150,000 francs. Pasdeloup, who came to congratulate him, went on to say: 'Your *Credo,* Monsieur l'Abbé, is a sure success for popular concerts.'

After further not very eventful travels, Liszt returned to Rome where he spent Christmas. He wrote to the Princess that he had prayed especially for her at midnight mass, and that he 'should be made worthy of the supernatural sentiments' she showered upon him. However, the ceaseless squabbles continued. 'You no longer take any account of the logical honesty of my life,' he wrote to Carolyne. 'When I am dead, you will appreciate that my soul was and remains always deeply attached to yours.' The two elderly lovers were perpetually poised between the settling of accounts and sublime considerations.

1879   Practically the whole of this year was spent in Rome and Liszt worked hard. From four in the morning to midday he read, composed or meditated. In the afternoon, he would give piano lessons. He was now writing a new version of the 'Mephisto' Waltz, *Via crucis* and *Septem sacramenta.* There was always this contrast between work such

*Canon Liszt
(caricature by Borsszem Jankó, 1879).*

as 'Mephisto' and the mystical work representing the disembodied spirit of contemplation.

Also at this time Liszt discovered the work of the younger Russian musicians. The ardent defender of the music of the future awoke with enthusiasm to salute such innovations. Referring to Rimsky-Korsakov, Balakirev, Borodin, César Cui and Liadov, he says: 'These five musicians are ploughing a more fertile furrow than the backward imitators of Mendelssohn and Schumann.'

And for much of the time, he prayed. On 12 October he was made Canon of Albano, which entitled the venerable Franciscan dandy to wear the purple sash, the supreme coquetry to which photographs of the time bear witness.

1880   Liszt may well have written: 'The weariness of age and a kind of inner sadness, the fruit of a too long experience, are increasing and making public appearances extremely painful for me,' but every so often the travel demon would enter into him again. This year there were further journeys across Europe, then a season at Weimar, and a long stay at the Budapest conservatoire, where he was the constant

Wagner at home by Beckmann, 1880.

companion of a very young woman, Lina Schmalhausen, his last experience of gallantry. But Lina's rôle was more that of companion than of flirt, for Liszt's health was beginning to give him some trouble in the form of an incipient dropsy, which he sedulously refused to treat other than by his habitual glass of cognac.

 1881 In the spring, Liszt composed a thirteenth symphonic poem – the only one not dedicated to the Princess – *From the Cradle to the Grave*, a score which clearly lacks the vigour of his great period. He also did some work this year on the *Cantico del sol di San Francesco d'Assisi*.

In July he left for Weimar, but not to work very much. His health was becoming more and more delicate and he suffered from sleepiness and fatigue. One day he had a bad fall on the stairs and took a long time to recover, despite the devoted attentions of Bülow and his daughter Daniela, who never left him. Borodin, who was passing through Weimar, came very shyly to call on him. But Liszt encouraged him, congratulating him on the boldness of his modulations, and telling him how hopeful he was of the future of the young Russian school.

Liszt's convalescent period was spent at Bayreuth, where Cosima stayed with him for the whole month of September, while Wagner completed *Parsifal* in an adjoining room.

In October, accompanied by his granddaughter Daniela, Liszt left for Rome. On the morning of his birthday, the 22nd, he received from Carolyne the following letter:

'Dear, dear friend, may your seventieth birthday begin under the auspices of the sun which will shine on 22 October at Woronince. Let us breathe eternity. It was for eternity that I desired to possess you in God and to give you to God. May you have a happy year and many happy years, dear great one. You have great things to do. And God who gives the wherewithal to do them also gives the reward here below as well as hereafter. As we await the final recompense, let us rejoice in what little we have here and now ... au revoir. Saint Francis has worked so many miracles, he will work some for you, too, who are covering him with glory. Secular glory.'

That same day, on which a small party had been organised by Liszt's Roman friends, he had a telegram from Wagner: 'You gave her life (he is referring to Cosima); you gave me back to life. As long as you spread goodness and beauty around you — and you will never be able to do otherwise — this life remains yours and we offer it to you with all our gratitude. Greetings to you! Your friend.' Liszt wrote back immediately: 'My one and only friend, today, 22 October, your poem brings me a profound and unspeakable joy. May no delusion, but peace and joy be with you, Cosima and the children. In all fidelity, your Franciscus.' The last sentence refers to the German words *Wahn* (delusion) and *Fried* (peace) which Wagner had used for the name of his house at Bayreuth.

1882   Winter in Rome went by with few notable events. But in spring came a beautiful message — the score of *Parsifal* with the dedication: 'Oh, my friend, my Franz, the first and only one, receive this gift of thanks from your Richard Wagner.' And Liszt replied immediately, copying out in his own hand a theme from the work:

'With the bell-chimes of your *Parsifal* . . .

your kindred spirit thanks you for ever and from the bottom of his heart!'

Despite his persistently frail health, Liszt spent his traditional seasons at Weimar and Budapest that year. Then in August he went to Bayreuth to attend the first performance of *Parsifal*. The work won his fullest admiration, a fact which did not fail to irritate Carolyne yet again. He wrote:

'My point of view remains the same, absolute admiration, excessive if you like. *Parsifal* is more than a masterpiece, it is a revelation in musical drama. It has been justly said that after the Song of Songs of earthly love which is *Tristan and Isolde,* Wagner has created in *Parsifal* the supreme song of heavenly love.'

He stayed with the Wagners for the whole of the latter part of the year. First, he attended the wedding of his granddaughter Blandine. Then, in October, everyone moved to Venice to the Palazzo Vendramino. Their time was devoted to family life, except that Liszt got to work again on his *Saint Stanislaus*. Every morning he went to mass, and read a great deal, too. He was certainly not lacking in courage for he launched into the twenty-two interminable (and unfinished) volumes of the Princess's 'Causes'. But he also hastened to report to her his lack of success in assimilating them.

'What an immense labour are these 22 volumes of the 'Causes'. Truly, you spring from Saint Augustine, Saint Bernard, Saint Thomas, Saint Theresa, Saint Catherine of Siena — and a little also from Joseph de Maistre for, do not be displeased, you share with him his militant, prophetic sense .... Indeed, I understand nothing of politics or theology; with the result that three quarters of your labour remains above my head. As to the aesthetic side, I must confess as well that I have not so far found the Ariadne's thread which will lead me out of the maze of these numerous systems of ancient and modern philosophy. Let us hope that I shall finally seize upon the right thread in your enlightened theory of emotions and sensations. Until then, I see myself condemned to sceptical grief.'

At the end of his stay, before leaving for Budapest, Liszt wrote *La Gondole funèbre*.

1883   On 14 February, in the morning, Liszt learned of the death of Wagner. Liszt was in his room, writing, when someone came to tell him the news. He had a strange reaction. At first he went on writing, and made no response. Then, a long moment afterwards, he murmured: 'Why not?' Then he remained silent for some time, and, looking up at last, said: 'They have buried me, too, many times.' Shortly afterwards, a telegram arrived from Daniela: 'Mama asks you not to come. Stay quietly at Pest. We shall bring the body back to Bayreuth after a short stay at Munich.' 'He today, I tomorrow,' said Liszt simply, thinking that dying was simpler than living and that there alone is 'our deliverance from an unwilling yoke, the consequence of original sin'.

Liszt stayed at Budapest until May and then went on to Weimar where, despite bad health and his worsening dropsy, he was to participate in a great memorial service, during the course of which he conducted *Good Friday music* as well as a work composed by him for the occasion: *Am Grabe Richard Wagners*.

He then left for Budapest, to prepare a new version of his *Requiem*.

1884   A quiet year during which all the contrasting elements of Liszt's personality are manifested: meditative and solitary moods alternate with the need for activity and travel. In the spring he conducted fragments of the famous *Saint Stanislaus*, which he was never to finish at Weimar. In August, at Bayreuth, he heard *Parsifal*. Cosima,

The return of the prodigal son, Hungary 18

shut up in fierce mourning, refused even to see him. In September he made a tour of Hungary where peasants and princes alike gave him the usual triumphal welcome.

Worn out, he arrived back in Rome towards autumn.

1885 Once the New Year celebrations were over Liszt went off again – this time just as he did in his youth – to roam Europe giving concerts in Italy, Austria, Holland, France, Germany, Hungary. The usual visits were made to Weimar and Budapest. It is curious to note that this was one of the most active years of his career. Moreover, he composed on the edges of tables, in hotel bedrooms. 'I am more or less deliberately wasting time. With the feebleness of old age, work is getting difficult; but I continue to labour at blackening manuscript paper.' He returned to Rome towards the end of the year in a state of great fatigue.

With Lina Schmalhausen.

1886   This last year of Liszt's life was no less active and agitated than
the previous one. The great traveller was to light one last firework. At
the beginning of January he launched a series of concerts devoted to his

99

music. These were to be his last public performances as a pianist.

Then he took off again on what he called his 'supreme grand tour'. First Italy (Florence and Venice), then Austria (Vienna). Delirious crowds greeted him everywhere. Triumphal galas were organised. He was acclaimed, smothered in flowers and honours. Outrageous propositions were made to him, some by relatively quiet women who wanted simply to look after him, others from those who were offering him a great deal more. He then stopped at Liège, where a similar welcome awaited him, before going on to Paris, where he was to fall a prey to turbulent admirers and where his 'Gran' Mass was to be performed twice at Saint Eustache, with triumphant success. Then London, where he led a very distinguished life, received by the royal family and attending a very fine performance of his *St. Elisabeth*. It was now April and he had already travelled a great deal since the beginning of the year. But, paying no attention to his weariness, he went on. During Holy Week he arrived at Antwerp and was back again in Paris by the first week in May, attending a performance of the *St. Elisabeth* conducted at the Trocadero by Colonne in front of an audience of six thousand. 'It is constructed on holy stones', cried Gounod.

In June Liszt visited Weimar and in July Bayreuth, where he arrived almost completely exhausted to attend the wedding of his granddaughter Daniela to a young writer, Thode, author of a remarkable work on St. Francis of Assisi which Liszt had actually just read. But this was not to be the last journey. There was one more, this time to Luxemburg, where an old friend, the Hungarian painter Munkacsy, had invited him. He left there again on 20 July for Bayreuth, caught a cold in the train and, on arrival in Bayreuth, went to bed with a high fever. He was living in a little house near Wahnfried. Unable to rest, he made every effort to get up on 22 July in order to visit Cosima. But his strength failed and he had to stay in bed. The friends he had there came to visit him or played whist with him. And once again he got up.

Saturday, 24th: He received pupils and visited Wahnfried.

Sunday 25th: Despite doctor's orders to the contrary, he had himself carried into Wagner's box for a complete performance of *Tristan.*

100

Liszt's funeral.

Monday 26th: A relapse. He was forbidden even the brandy he took to revive himself, and his strength waned considerably.

Tuesday 27th: The chill became a serious pulmonary congestion and the doctor prescribed absolute rest, with no visitors. Cosima had a bed made up for herself outside his room.

101

Wednesday 28th: complete prostration.

Thursday 29th: complete prostration.

Friday 30th: Delirium.

Saturday 31st: At two in the morning, an even more terrible crisis point in his delirium. While unconscious, Liszt regained a frightening new strength, crying out, getting out of bed and jostling the servant who tried to get him back. At about eight o'clock the doctor came to give him an injection and later Cosima asked if he wished to see a priest. 'Nothing . . . no-one', murmured Liszt. The whole of the day he remained quiet, except for a moment when he was heard to stammer: 'Tristan'. When, during the evening, Cosima asked if he was suffering, he whispered: 'Not any more', and in the middle of the night he died quietly.

As he had asked, his funeral arrangements were very simple and without music. Not a poor man's burial, as he would have liked, but it was in fact a poor man who had died. Liszt left as his sole legacy his soutane, a few shirts and seven handkerchiefs.

He was laid to rest in Bayreuth cemetery.

A matinée at Liszt's house (from l. to r. Berlioz, Cze Liszt, and the violinist Ernst) by Kriehuber, 1846.

LISZT AND THE PIANO

That Liszt created modern piano technique is an historical truth which no-one would dispute, although musical literature has less to say on this point than its paramount importance might suggest. It is also worth observing at this stage that Liszt's enormous piano output is very incompletely known to the public and very poorly made use of by performers. Apart from a few bravura pieces, always the same ones, the bulk of this output, which of course is not without its weaknesses, has been most unjustly neglected.

Within his gigantic output for the piano — in which there exist several very different versions of certain compositions — we can detect the three essential aspects in the transcendent technician, thanks to whom the potential of the instrument and the faculties of the instrumentalist were extended at least tenfold (and this is appreciable even if one makes a comparison with Chopin, or with certain deliberately specialised passages of Schumann). Then we have the romantic musician, the creator of free programme music, first cousin to those impressionists who have cropped up throughout the history of French music (and it has already been remarked upon that a whole area of his piano work is a sort of trial run preceding the creation of the symphonic poem). Finally, there is the composer of pure music — not on the whole a Lisztian speciality — with works like the sonata or the two concertos. Thus his output for the piano can be said to provide a fairly complete picture of Liszt's creative versatility.

For the purposes of clarity, this output can be categorised under five major headings:

1. *Études* or exercises
2. Transcriptions and paraphrases
3. Works of a purely folk music
4. Original creative works in the sphere of programme or similar music
5. Original creative works in the sphere of pure music or the like.

Saint-Saëns, when speaking of Liszt's piano music, writes very truly (despite the numerous aesthetic stupidities he has been known to commit) that in spite of the apparent paradox. Liszt had a greater influence where the piano is concerned than Paganini with the violin, 'Paganini remained in an inaccessible position where he alone could survive, whereas Liszt, from the same point of departure, condescended to the realm of practical consideration where anyone who is prepared to take the trouble to work seriously can follow him. And it was again Saint-Saëns who made the absolutely correct observation:

'As against Beethoven, who held in contempt the limitations of the body and imposed his tyrannical will on overworked and frustrated fingers, Liszt takes those fingers and exercises them naturally so as to obtain the maximum effect of which they are capable without doing violence to them. Thus his music, frightening as it is at first sight to the timid, is in reality less difficult than it appears.'

Obviously, it was easy for a virtuoso such as Saint-Saëns, who had 'worked seriously', and who was endowed with considerable gifts, to adopt this point of view. But it is a fact that Liszt's technique is a natural one, meaning that it takes into account the hand's natural physical potential.

The interesting and original thing about Liszt's contribution is the

105

way he carried the development of this natural potential to its limits, which he exalted to the full, exploiting their power. He is not a revolutionary of keyboard technique, but he is an innovator of genius in that he has increased the fund of pianistic effects, and not only the sound but also the mechanics, rhythm and dynamics. Liszt, as we know, was never a man of the theatre. The only opera he attempted — as a mere child, it is true — gives no sign of a special gift in that respect. But, throughout his life, he treated the piano in the manner of a great dramatist of the keyboard. Liszt's piano is the piano of drama. And it was in order to meet the demands of this dynamic, expressive, dramatic quality that he invented the prodigious and original technique which, at the same time as proving itself heir to the findings of the later Beethoven, and Weber, is nonetheless entirely new, with its wealth of hitherto unknown sound effects, its chord themes, its doublings and double notes, its very particular effects with octaves, the wide musical texture his music assumes on the keyboard, that complex, polyphonic, almost orchestral sumptuousness, that tightly-woven, dense texture. Leaps over long intervals, pizzicati, glissandi, tremolos, brilliant double-note phrases, high-trills imitating the cymbalon, dovetailing or cross-over of hands and that habit of producing a strong singing inner part by alternating between thumbs, and so on — all this was absolutely new, transforming the character of the piano and consequently that of piano music and opening the door to all the great innovations, all the great compositions to come in the modern keyboard music of such composers as Albeniz, Debussy, Stravinsky, Prokofiev, Bartok and Schoenberg. With Liszt one experiences a complete liberation of piano techniques for the apparently paradoxical reason that, except in special cases, he is not using technique for its own sake but for the sake of music. And this is also why, right up to the beginning of the twentieth century, teachers (traditionalists as they were for the most part) were suspicious of Liszt. The great Marmontel was particularly lacking in understanding on this score. Liszt upset all their habits. Such a broadening of the scope of music by the liberation of technique made their heads spin and introduced a disagreeable element of confusion into their tiny routine.

It is clear also that not only did Liszt liberate the mechanics of the instrument in the name of music, but also musical form. He was anxious above all to make form serve ideas, to find, for each thought, the particular, unique formal means of expressing it, with no regard for academic convention. Liszt's greatness lay above all in his refusal to follow convention, inventing for himself, both in the sphere of sound and in that of architectonics, means adequate to the translation of his thought. In this way he opened wide the door to the aesthetic liberalism which has characterised the evolution of modern music.

It is impossible here to embark upon arid details such as an examination of Liszt's pianistic technique would entail. There is no alternative but to stick to generalities.

However, certain special points should be noted which too often tend to be overlooked. As was observed earlier, Liszt was not so much a revolutionary in keyboard technique as a brilliant innovator. In fact it does not appear that Liszt wanted to break with the essential traditions of those who had gone before, in particular Beethoven. But the innovations in piano technique which he introduced with such calm and regal audacity did border on the revolutionary. It has also been observed that in the field of expression he resembled a dramatist of the piano. One might also add that, in the field of pure technique, he showed himself to be a symphonist of the keyboard. Even before the modern concert hall, that is a hall containing several hundred, even several thousand listeners came into being, he was composing for it. With a veritable genius for finger work (such as was possible but not always easy at that time) he created that style of orchestral piano playing which is one of the characteristics (and not always an absolutely happy one) of modern piano playing – a style which brings to the instrument all its potential proportions and repercussions of sound.

Liszt created a new physical concept in piano playing. Czerny, and even Chopin in his *Études,* had to a certain extent remained tied to the measured smoothness of the harpsichord, playing with the hands relatively close to the keyboard. Liszt changed all this. His style brought elbows, shoulders and chest into play (and as a result interpretation of Chopin's work was enriched, for although the latter had great musical foresight, he had not applied this on the physical level

107

of keyboard technique). With Liszt we encounter completely new combinations, which Scarlatti may have foreseen, but which only Liszt accomplished fully — with his great jumps from chord to chord, his hands streaking up and down the keys, astonishing the audiences of the day as much as the clusters of notes Boulez plucks from his instrument do now. As to the use of the pedal, he showed reckless daring for the period, daring which was contrary to all the rules of harmony of the time, heralding the richness of the sound palette of those composers known as the French impressionists, of the beginning of the twentieth century.

He also had a way of 'registering' piano music, consisting of the left hand playing great, mellow, harmonic bass notes, with the right hand playing brilliant decorations with a flying touch, while the thumbs played the melody in the middle register. (This manner of having the thumbs play the melody — either alternately or not — is a familiar thing with Liszt, and he even applied it to the music of other composers when he could, for instance in the finale of Chopin's Sonata in B minor.) Finally, we can only briefly point out here some of the forms of virtuosity which astounded people at the time by their boldness: frenzied glissandi of thirds and sixths as in the transcription of Berlioz's *Symphonie fantastique,* long trills of a harmonic nature in the upper ranges of the keyboard, hands crossed, hands interlaced, etc . . . all things which were extremely daring at the time and even appeared extravagant, since they upset the traditions of classical piano playing.

I will now briefly survey the different pianistic forms, as already outlined, and then make a concise analysis of one of the most significant pages of the Sonata in B minor.

The Études or Exercises

As we saw from Liszt's biography, we are here faced with two kinds of works. The first consists of keyboard adaptations of Paganini's six *Caprices* for the violin. The very famous *La Campanella* appears in this collection. Liszt was motivated by a spirit of rivalry with respect to the 'infernal violinist', and it is because of this that the *Études* display what was at the time a stupendous daring and incredible innovation in instrumental technique. All the discoveries of Lisztian pianistic style are in these *Études* which, besides being masterpieces of acrobatics, are the result of the most elevated and powerful inspiration (although Schumann, who had also written *Études*, treated them rather off-handedly), and contain all the innovations of Liszt's piano style.

Liszt at the piano by Danhauser, 1840 (l. to r. A. Dumas, Victor Hugo, George Sand, Paganini, Rossini, Liszt and Mme. d'Agoult; Beethoven's bust on the piano, Byron behind Rossini)

'Chromatic galop by the Devil of harmony'
(caricature by Lablache and Haberneck, 1843).

As a whole they present two main types: on the one hand those which seem to aim at reproducing characteristic violin effects for the keyboard, and on the other hand those in which, prompted by an extraordinary daring and inventiveness, Liszt sets out to demonstrate, as it were, that the piano's resources are greater than the violin's.

The second series is composed of the *Études d'exécution transcendante,* which are wholly Liszt's work and not composed from borrowed themes. In these *Études,* which probably still represent the summit of the development of keyboard technique, the Romantic artist also appears, inspired by literature and poetry. This is the earliest form of the embryo from which there emerged, after the other piano works, these pyrotechnics of programme music, of which Liszt was to become one of the heroes. These *Études* have names, for they are, in effect, programmatic and were inspired, as to their poetic content, either by his own impressions or by literature. They have names like *Harmonies du soir*, one of the most profoundly poetic, or *Paysage*, which has a simple charm, or again *Feux-follets*, famous for its sparkling style, or finally *Mazeppa*, a truly dramatic piece which he later drew upon to compose the symphonic poem of the same name.

Transcriptions and Paraphrases

Here once again a desire for the greatest virtuosity governs these pages and one is obliged to say that most of them cannot seriously be considered among the best works left by Liszt. They are of two kinds. First, transcriptions of *lieder* – Schubert, Beethoven, Schumann, Mendelssohn, etc. – and the paraphrases of operas – *Lucia di Lammermoor, Robert le Diable, Don Giovanni, Rigoletto* as well as endless lesser-known works.

From a technical point of view they may be interesting, ingenious or even amusing but they do not have the same qualities on a strictly musical level. They are often sacrificed to the taste – one might even say the bad taste – of a period when people enjoyed this sort of brilliant fantasy based on popular melodies. Sometimes they are not even justifiable musically, especially the *lieder* transcriptions, in which Liszt takes great liberties with the original texts and, under the pretext of making up for lack of words, introduces innumerable decorations, *fioritures* and brilliant acrobatic cadenzas, all intended to enhance the performer's technique and to lend a very debateable variety to the treatment of the musical ideas. These variants – not conceived of as variations, as has been wrongly held, but solely as decoration – often falsify the profound nature of the original work.

Again, as regards the opera transcriptions, one shudders a little at the mentality of a pianist who, amid rapturous applause, plays a Fantasy on an air by Meyerbeer as an encore to a concert devoted to Beethoven Sonatas.

The transcriptions of organ and orchestral works are included under the same heading. These are infinitely more serious from a musical point of view. The transcriptions of the Preludes and Fugues for Organ by J.S. Bach are very fine, diligently faithful to Bach's ideas, and have

111

the priceless advantage of making these incomparable masterpieces available to pianists.

The transcriptions of orchestral works have one serious drawback; they are often impossibly difficult to play. This applies in particular to the nine Beethoven Symphonies, to Berlioz's *Symphonie fantastique* and *Harold in Italy,* and Liszt was probably the only one able to perform them at concerts. But the piano rendition is extraordinarily rich and almost symphonic in tone, and such is Liszt's skill and ingenuity that one has a constant impression of orchestral detail.

All of this makes these transcriptions the most fascinating documents. Here again, the potential of keyboard technique was expanded.

I should add that the works under this heading are not, however, solely of a mechanical or even dynamic interest. It has become fashionable from a musical point of view to treat these transcriptions and paraphrases with contempt. Certainly some of them have the undeniable flaws of the period, and some of them are like certain of the *Études,* at which Schumann levelled the following, just, criticism – since he knew perfectly well through personal experience just what 'transcendental studies' were. He wrote:

'If we examine several pages of these collected works closely, we find the essence of the music on which they are based is undeniably out of all proportion to the technical difficulties involved. But here the word *Études* covers a multitude of sins; it is a matter of practice at any cost.'

One might paraphrase the last sentence and say of the collected works we are concerned with here: 'They are a matter of brillance at any cost.'

Having said this, one ought not to exaggerate. Although most of the paraphrases of Italian opera were forgotten (many of them quite unjustly), this was often because the operas themselves were no longer performed, being considered very old-fashioned or dated. But today, now that famous Italian singers such as Tebaldi or Callas or di Stefano and others have made this kind of repertoire fashionable once more, and it is no longer considered absurd to go and hear *Norma* or *Lucia di*

Lammermoor, these transcriptions and paraphrases will no doubt be judged less harshly. Some young pianists are not afraid to add them to their repertoire and have already made some very lively recordings, showing how very unjust their elders were.

In treating this part of Liszt's works with contempt, the argument was often advanced that this was only bread and butter entertainment, an almost accidental part of his output, and that on the whole, Liszt's share in their creation was almost non-existent. This is not so. On the one hand, these 'entertainments' recur rather consistently all through Liszt's life and although the years 1830-1845 were the most prolific in this field, one must not forget that right up to 1880, Liszt went on paraphrasing such people as Meyerbeer, Gounod and Tchaikovsky. Secondly, Wagner himself — who had no particular liking for this sort of exercise — nevertheless recognised that Liszt's creative share was undeniable, in these just as elsewhere: 'This wonderful man,' he wrote, 'can do nothing without giving his heart and soul to the work in hand. Not content with reproducing, he could never undertake any activity unless it were productive. In him, everything tends towards pure creation.' These statements are easily verified. Remarkable analyses of *Réminiscences de Lucia di Lammermoor* and *Réminiscences de La Norma* by André Schaeffner have proved this beyond all shadow of doubt. The first piece, obviously one of Liszt's finest, shows how the whole thing appears to be one of Liszt's compositions, and yet not a note, not a harmony, not an accent, was by him. Everything is faithfully transcribed from the sextet in Act II. Liszt simply enriched the arabesques in the accompaniment instead of keeping Donizetti's monotonous arpeggios. These demisemiquaver arabesques are broken up by trills which, within Donizetti's formal harmony, create a new dissonance, enough to modify the nature of the excerpt profoundly and to give it a typically Lisztian character. André Schaeffner remarks: 'A valuable lesson, since it proves how slight a foundation individuality in the arts rests on, how slender a technical basis it has, and since it shows us all that Donizetti and Liszt had in common both melodically and harmonically.'

He draws attention to a cadence in E flat minor in the same passage, where Donizetti and Liszt slow these bars down with the same

113

chromatic semi-tones and the same decorations. An E flat – F – A flat – E flat group (with B flat in the right hand arpeggio) heralds this passage with its obviously Lisztian, even Tristanesque sound, yet it remains the harmony Donizetti intended, with the subtle difference that on the piano it gathers itself on a low note that lends itself to the special appeal of a minor seventh doubled in the octave, and an open fifth.

There are many more examples. One day this might be a job worth undertaking not only for purely theoretical reasons, but above all to reassure nervous pianists who do not dare add these works to their repertoires; for these works would certainly not bring them into disrepute and would give them a splendid opportunity of demonstrating their talents.

The Hungarian Rhapsodies

No lengthy comment is needed on these. But given what Liszt said about them himself, and the slight misunderstanding that exists concerning them, a short restatement might be useful.

In his work *Des Bohémiens et de leur musique en Hongrie*, Liszt writes:

'I wanted to make a sort of national epic out of Gipsy music . . . the word "Rhapsody" was meant to indicate the fantastic, epic quality we believed it to have. Each of these works always seemed to me to belong to a poetic cycle. The extracts do not narrate any events, it is true, but ears that know how to listen will catch the expression of certain of those states of the soul in which a national ideal is summed up . . . . These Rhapsodies were called "Hungarian" because it would have been unjust to separate in the future what had not been separate in the past. The Magyars adopted the Bohemians as their national musicians . . . if the one needed singers, the others could not do without an audience. Hungary can therefore with justice claim as its own this art nourished by its wheat and vines, mellowed in its sun and shade . . . so interwoven in its customs that it is one with the land's most glorious memories, as well as the most personal recollections of every Hungarian.'

In fact, these Rhapsodies are not Hungarian at all; they are pure Gipsy music, just as are Brahms' famous Dances. But Liszt did not know this. By his time, genuine, native Magyar music had almost entirely disappeared, or at least it only existed in the depths of certain parts of the countryside. This is what two musicians, Béla Bartók and Zoltan Kodaly, were to show at the beginning of the twentieth century when they unearthed authentic Hungarian melodies and rhythms, whose appeal is very different from the Gipsy music that had exclusively inspired the conception and indeed the instrumental style of Liszt's Rhapsodies.

To be exact, it is worth remembering that Gipsy music may sometimes contain a Hungarian element. It often made use of the Hungarian pentatonic scale, since the Gipsies partially assimilate some of the characteristics of the countries they live in. But that is all. And if the intervals resemble those in Hungarian music of a Magyar origin, the melodies, rhythms and especially the instrumental style do not, the latter being essentially restrained, which is far from being the case in Gipsy music.

Having said this, Liszt's Hungarian Rhapsodies constitute yet further piano pyrotechnics, besides being particularly difficult to play because of their directly ethnic nature. The interesting thing about them lies in their enrichment of keyboard technique by a whole series of sound effects borrowed from typical Gipsy instruments, the violin and the cymbalon.

Original Creative Works (Programme Music)

These form the most important and interesting part of Liszt's piano works. In this field we should first mention those three great volumes of the *Années de pèlerinage;* the *Harmonies poétiques et religieuses,* the two *Légendes,* the Consolations, the *Ballades,* the *Polonaises* and the Variations on *Weinen, Klagen, Sorgen, Zagen* and even possibly pieces like the *Grand galop chromatique.*

The three books of the *Années de pèlerinage* (an infinitely finer title than that originally chosen, *Album d'un voyageur*) constitute thirty or o pieces in completely free form, varying in importance as well as in character, at times lyrical, at times programmatic and on a variety of

Excerpt from manuscript of sketches composed in 1875.

subjects according to whether they were inspired by nature, mankind or the arts. In the biography, we saw the circumstances in which these pieces were composed, some at the start and some at the end of Liszt's career.

We hear the great voices of nature (*Au lac de Wallenstadt, Pastorale, Au bord d'une source, Orage, Eglogue, Les cloches de Genève, Au cyprès de la Villa d'Este, Les jeux d'eau de la Villa d'Este,* or the additional pieces in the short Venetian and Neapolitan book), we come across a succession of artistic or historic heroes (*La Chapelle de Guillaume Tell, La vallée d'Obermann, Sposalizio* — inspired by Raphael's painting at La Brera — *Il penseroso* — a tribute to Michelangelo's statue of Giuliano de Medici in Florence — *Canzonetta del Salvator Rosa,* the three *Sonetti del Petrarca,* 'Dante' Sonata, *Marche funèbre* — a meditation in memory of Maximilian I, Emperor of Mexico). Some of the other pieces, without belonging to a programme and without being completely abstract, are in a sense impressionistic: *Le mal du pays, Angelus, Sunt lacrymae rerum, Sursum corda,* and even *Lyon.*

Of course, Liszt put his heart and soul into all this in the true Romantic manner. This is essentially poetic music, written at the whim of the composer-poet's fantasy and lacking any preconceived form. As was said earlier, this is the last stage in Liszt's development before he extended his art into the form of symphonic poem.

On this subject, it might be useful to let the author speak for himself:

'Having recently travelled through many new lands, many different sites, many places celebrated in history and poetry; having felt that the variegated aspects of nature and the scenery connected with it did not pass before my eyes as fruitless images, but rather that they stirred deep emotions within me, that a vague but direct relationship had sprung up between us, unidentified but real bonds, a sure but inexplicable communication, I attempted to render into music some of my most impassioned feelings, my keener perceptions .... As instrumental music advances, develops and throws off its early shackles, it tends to take on the same ideal quality that has marked the perfection of the plastic arts. It is no longer just a combination of sounds but a poetic language, perhaps even better able than poetry itself to express everything in us that extends beyond our usual horizons, everything that escapes analysis, is linked to inaccessible profundities, imperishable desires, measureless forebodings. Convinced of this, I undertook to write this work, appealing to the few rather than the many. Not aspiring to success but to the approbation of those few who see art as destined for something other than the amusement of a few idle hours, and demand ˙something else of it than the frivolous distraction of short-lived amusement.'

These lines are from the Preface to the first edition of *Années de pèlerinage* (Paris, 1841). Despite a few old-fashioned turns of phrase, these are some of the finest lines written on musical Romanticism. The Romantic attitude that views the world through the glass of one's personality, is clearly marked in the epigraph chosen by Liszt for one of his pieces, *Les cloches de Genève:*

> I live not in myself, but I become
> Portion of that around me.

> (Byron, *Child Harold*)

This is the guiding principle of the *Années de pèlerinage.*

Finally we should note that in many of these places Liszt is not always content with attempting to depict his own feelings but also, through them, he tries to paint the feelings of another, such as Byron or Senancour, which justifies the title, *Années de pèlerinage,* pilgrimages to places where others had suffered and loved.

Linked with the *Années de pèlerinage* and in the same vein are the two *Légendes: Saint François de Paule marchant sur les flots* and *Saint François d'Assise prêchant aux oiseaux.* These two are no longer simply impressionistic, but are sometimes almost descriptive.

Années de pèlerinage – very rarely played right through since the only pieces favoured by pianists are the brilliant virtuoso ones – is one of the most remarkable monuments of Romantic keyboard composition.

The Consolations are a small collection of short pieces – fairly easy

118

to play — which, on the contrary, do not seem to have any set plan, although they were inspired by some of the poems in the Sainte-Beuve collection of the same name. They tend rather towards the confidential intimacy of Schumann's style. Equally unjustly neglected, these Consolations are among the most moving pages left to us by the composer.

There are two versions of the Variations, one for organ, the other for piano. Their theme is one Bach used for one of his Cantatas — *Weinen, Klagen, Sorgen, Zagen* (Weeping, Sorrow, Fear, Timidity) — and they were written on the occassion of the inauguration of a Bach memorial. As Alfred Cortot has observed, Bach had treated this sorrowful, romantic theme as a Protestant, while Liszt:

'... found in this an expression of Catholicism and Catholic pomp. The impression of religious things is more fetishistic than Bach's. We also get a Dantesque feeling from them. Liszt not only makes use of the three sad words from the point of view of musical colour, but they allow him to make a transition, to cut from one to the other. The chorus "All that God hath made is well" which comes in at the most sorrowful moment, as if to break its terrible, severe domination, to show us the light, is a Protestant theme also used by Bach in the same cantata . . . . What a feeling of consolation and glorification this theme brings us, after the desperate waiting, the terror, the feeling of fatality and the threat which hung over us!'

Original Creative Works (Pure Music)

In this field, Liszt's great, original achievement is his Piano Sonata in B minor, dedicated to Robert Schumann. The Manifesto Liszt wrote shortly before the Sonata appeared concerning the publication of the Symphonic Poems introduced principles that were highly revolutionary for the period. This Sonata is a revolution of another kind. This is pure music in contrast to programme music. But it is the form, the method of treating a classic form in accordance with a quite new concept that is revolutionary.

At first sight, it appears to make a complete break with what even Beethoven had conceived of as advanced concepts. It is because of this

119

An Robert Schumann

Sonate

für das Piano-Forte —

von

F. Liszt —

that many musicologists and musicians feel Liszt's Sonata has retained its exceptionally disturbing character for so long. Until the beginning of the twentieth century, theoreticians such as Vincent d'Indy and Blanche Selva treated this masterpiece with scorn and contempt as not coming within the classic framework of this traditional and firmly catalogued *genre*. Yet what else had Liszt done but to give a new evolutionary impetus to a form which had already been in a continual state of evolution for one hundred years!

This is the zenith of Liszt's painistic achievement and in it he sometimes even exceeded the instrument's normal range. While its subject is quite different, the Sonata has the sort of scope of the Symphonic Poems, whose freedom of form, and whose breadth and orchestral grandeur it shares. It too reflects the basic concern which always remained with Liszt, not to rely on a pre-established formal framework, but on the contrary to find the special form to suit a particular musical concept. In this sense, Rietsch wrote with good reason that, thanks to the symphonic poem, the Sonata freed itself by fusing its different movements in one whole.

Then again, this work is probably to represent the dramatic pinnacle of Liszt's piano music, for it has a drama not even attained in his Variations on *Weinen, Klagen, Sorgen, Zagen,* thrilling though they are in that respect.

The thing which has struck people and shocked them most is the fact that the Sonata has only one huge, twenty-five minute movement. Gone are the three or four traditional sections of Haydn, Mozart or Beethoven, a scheme which Schubert, Schumann and Brahms revived. In the arrangement of this single, deliberately unified movement, we do not even find the normal, classical, symmetrical arrangement of exposition – development – recapitulation. In the same way, we do not find the accepted tonal progressions which are the rule with Beethoven, even in his freest moments.

To tell the truth, despite its new look, it did not break with the past completely. Thanks to its thematic treatment and the arrangement of its themes, it does have a certain 'cyclical' pattern, which is nothing like the strictly cyclical form employed later by César Franck and developed until it became a mania with some of his successors, despite the fact that it is already anticipated in Beethoven's last sonatas. It is easy to see that Liszt's Sonata is close to Beethoven's last sonatas on another level; namely the psychological conception of the work, something which ought not to have escaped all those who have denigrated it with such remorseless stupidity. In fact, Beethoven had used the bithematic principle of the classical sonata as a dialogue or a dramatic struggle. Liszt devoted the same spirit to it while freely exploiting the form to its utmost.

Two opposing elements are evident from the very start of the work, which opens with a seven bar Lento, an introduction in the nature of a sombre meditation, written on the descending Hungarian scale:

This Lento leads into an 'allegro energico' where the two main themes are stated immediately after each other. The first is violent, headstrong, abrupt:

then the second theme appears without any transition; it is brusque and sarcastic:

After a long silence, a violent struggle between these two themes begins producing a striking contrast with the manner in which they were introduced. This struggle is a battle to the death, wild beasts in combat, and in the development, neither one nor the other are victorious, both retaining their aggressive quality right the way through. Yet the first theme remains dominant, asserting itself in a lightning-like passage of staccato octaves. Then a sort of dark, grandiose coda concludes the opening and we now hear the initial theme of the descending, Hungarian scale, harmonised.

This coda introduces a 'grandioso' episode, a full, slow movement, very solemn, based on a new lyrical, very warm theme, with an extremely thick texture:

Then the first theme reappears, only this time it is treated melodically, 'dolce con grazia', rich in arpeggios. Thus it unfolds, mellow until the sarcastic theme breaks back in. Suddenly the sarcastic theme itself is transformed into a suave theme, a sort of nocturne accompanied by triple arpeggios. This nocturne is developed at length right up to the piano cadence, where the trills merge.

Then the vigorous struggle between the two opening themes begins once again with Liszt displaying all the contrapuntal means at his command (augmentation, diminution, inversion, contrary motion, etc.). Then comes a new, vibrant, brilliant and dynamic development of great virtuosity, crossed at times by the initial descending scale. After this, a new octave episode emerges from the opening theme and the fleeting but powerful 'grandioso' theme bursts out in great chords followed by a short recitative on a pattern born of the first theme, the repetition of the 'grandioso' chords, and a further recitative. An incisive episode based on the sarcastic theme takes over, largely overshadowed by the chords of the first theme. This leads to a short, melodic 'andante sostenuto', both introspective and tender in feeling, which serves as an introduction to a 'quasi adagio' which sings a 'dolcissimo con intimo sentimento' on a figure from the second theme. After a short cadenza, the 'grandioso' theme reappears, now treated with pathos and followed by a new development which ends sombrely with the return of the opening scale, then this in turn mysteriously dies out on two low F's as if struck on the timpani.

Suddenly, an 'allegro energico' begins, a fugue on two themes, none other than the two main themes, which follow one another after the abrupt exposition, ringing out like an exchange of violent, aggressive, sharp retorts. This fugal development is very rich in invention and combinations of all kinds. It also introduces the technique of variation, enlivened, moreover, by its extraordinarily dramatic dynamics. After a brief passage cut across in a menacing way by the opening descending scale, the development begins once again, the two initial themes come face to face and clash, the first in a passage of precipitato octaves, the second in unison in an imperious fortissimo. The 'grandioso' theme returns, more impressive than ever. Then the nocturne begins anew, reproduced with variants, becoming more and more animated, and terminating in an energetic 'stretta quasi presto', 'con strepido', based on the second theme. The opening descending scale flashes in a presto. A figure from the first theme crackles by in a 'prestissimo fuocoso assai', reintroducing the 'grandioso' motif once more. After a great crescendo enforced by a powerful tremolo in the right hand, there is sudden silence, then a brief 'andante sostenuto' episode, tender and introspective, leading to a few bars of an 'allegro moderato' which brings back the sarcastic theme, 'sotto voce', seeming to grate mysteriously in the background while the first theme, now serene, hovers over it again. The work ends on a 'lento assai', the sombre opening descending Hungarian scale capped with heavenly chords in the high register, while a low B, like a dull note on the timpani adds the final touch to this extraordinary piano epic, truly unique in the history of sound.

Liszt composed only one Sonata, but it is the work of a man who knew his *Faust* and *Divina Commedia* intimately.

There is no room here to emphasise everything which, beginning with this sonata (more than any other), Wagner owes to Liszt, particularly on a harmonic level, and how much Ravel's *Gaspard de la Nuit* absorbed from Liszt on a pianistic level.

A Student's Diary
Extracts from a diary kept in 1832
by Valerie Boissier, one of Liszt's
pupils.

'He played us an *Étude* by Moscheles.

"Would you like to try it?" he gracefully asked. "It is by one of my friends."

He played it delightfully, easily, in a rippling movement, a reverie, something inspired, soft, tender, unexpected yet naive, altogether enchanting . . . .

Before asking Valerie to begin this Étude, he read her Hugo's Ode to Jenny. In this way he wanted to make her understand the spirit of the piece, which he found so similar to that of poetry . . . .

He is profoundly humble before Weber and Beethoven. He says he is not yet fit to play them, yet he plays them, setting the piano on fire. He is so generous and kind that, seeing I had no liking for Herz, he played me a charming piece without telling me who it was by and, after I had enjoyed it, he took great pleasure in telling me the composer's name, yet Herz is his rival in musical glory. Natural abandon and unbridled passion is the master's motto. He is candid in everything he plays . . . .

Evidently Liszt searches after all sorts of emotions. He visits hospitals, gambling houses, lunatic asylums. He goes into the cells. He has even seen condemned men. He is a young man who thinks a great deal, who dreams, who delves into everything. His mind is as practised and as extraordinary as his hands and if he had not been a skilled musician, he would have been a philosopher or a distinguished man of letters . . . .

Liszt told us he had played the piano for years and had shone at concerts and thought himself a prodigy. Then one day, still unable to express all the feelings which oppressed him, he took stock of himself, tested himself bit by bit, finding he did not know how to play trills, or octaves or even read certain chords. From then on he had begun studying scales again and little by little had almost completely changed his fingering . . . .

He finds that rounded fingers produce a certain still style that he abhors; everything must be free, easy, unrestrained and effortless. His manner of expression is like his touch, natural and unpretentious. A passionate soul, fiery but naive, simple, tender, changeable, at times wrapped in despair, then in tenderness, then storm-tossed by love or jealousy, then weary and dejected; his music breathes this, according to Liszt. I said to him:

"To play well, you need to be sad."

"I am no longer capable of experiencing sadness."

"Perhaps anger, then."

"Base feelings could never gain ascendancy over me."

"Yes, your music is that of a good man."

He understood me and thanked me with his eyes . . . .

He is now busy re-educating himself and despite his inconceivable musical talent, I do not think he is destined to stay a musician and an artist. The prejudices that weigh on musical artists eat into his soul, and this to him is a crime. He is therefore attempting to escape from it. Furthermore, equipped with such rare intellectual faculties, he knows his own ability, he loves study, and will take gigantic steps forward in his career because he is on the right track. Already his conversation is fuller and shows more knowledge than a host of men who have completed their studies. He says appropriate things on a host of subjects. He has read a great deal, very wisely and he remembers it all.

He told me that for a long time he used to browse fruitlessly through books, then he began reading in a different way, re-reading what struck him most, often comparing books, and he finally believed he now set about it usefully. Whether it is literature or music, he is the same . . . .

He declaims the lines of a song close to his heart, the real thing, without any pretentiousness or charlatanism or little tricks for effect; he despises them. He says the thing as he feels it, truthfully, sincerely, unaffectedly . . . . His hands, gentle and flexible, rest on the instrument . . . this is the secret of his playing . . . .

We arrived at Liszt's at two and waited some minutes. I believe he was getting ready for we found him more elegantly dressed than usual. He had an air, a slight nuance of self-conceit, veiled by a background of kindness, a certain friendliness towards us and a great deal of politeness. He was pale and seemed uplifted, indifferent, but his eyes shone as much as usual and it was with real pleasure, perhaps even secret triumph, that little by little, without hurrying, he had his little say and recounted his success and pleasures in society since our last lesson. He had been to hear the best music in all Paris, he had dined with men of letters, had spent the whole night at balls, pursuing a fascinating young woman who was radiant with beauty and glamour, and had been married only a short while before to an elderly man. Her lovely Neapolitan eyes had fascinated him, and he had gazed on them from midnight until three o'clock . . . . He told us all this with a certain style; slowly, calmly, unexcitedly, without hurrying at all. His mother entered and the conversation broke off . . . . '

The Master Plays
Extract from an article signed by
A. Guemer in the first number of
the *Gazette Musicale* (5 January,
1834).

'We must now speak of a man for whom performance is everything, comprising as it does all the drama and lyricism, and all the artist's poetry. I refer, of course, to Liszt. In fact, if in Ferdinand Hiller we find knowledge, and the most sustained, the most profound embellishment of taste; in Bertini, inspiration and patience; in Chopin, the most exquisite sensitivity evidenced in physical terms; Liszt, the glorious pinnacle of this talented triangle, is above all especially a genius in performance. More than any other, he offers us an example of the path we must follow to make poetry of a form. For Liszt is not the result of a method, nor the evolution of special studies. Exercises can teach the hands to move over the keys swifter than the eye, to play those more or less held notes, these reserved pauses or movements, the absurd conventions of meretricious expression, empirical methods of exhibiting artistic truth or false sentimentality. But this deep concern for unknown work, this shining interpretation by which performance rises to the heights of creative genius, could only come out in a noble being, raised at once by all its faculties to the height of art in general. Liszt did not choose the hour of his birth, he was fated to be born in this day and age. The general movements of the century engendered him along with its other emancipations. Besides, sarcasm has been levelled in vain against this young, true talent. Liszt conquers envy in the same way as he has conquered his instrument. But do you know where he found such power? Liszt turned his attention to all the higher regions of the mind and seeing that literature, the theatre, philosophy and even science were being reborn in freedom, he followed in their footsteps in order to turn all the richness of the intellectual world to profit in his art. Undoubtedly this is Liszt's secret: If he interprets Beethoven so wonderfully, this is because he understands Shakespeare, Goethe, Schiller and Hugo. He understands the genius who composed *Fidelio* as well as he understands his works; Liszt is Beethoven's own hand.

Doubtless through the persistence of properly directed efforts, reaching beyond the purely mechanical and overcoming all difficulty, Liszt has turned his hands into an admirable voice, responsive to the most delicate inflexions of his soul. But it is with the additional support of the powerful wing of poetry that he has won for the performance of music a link tying it into that chain of ideality by which the arts rise and are joined to the heavens.

From now on this link will be a distinctive sign, among true artists and musical craftsmen. For soon, no doubt, it will be clear to all that composition is to musical performance, as form is to literature and colour is to painting. And just as poetry is only great and complete when the poet's thought and form are fused in the one, same beauty, in the same way performance reaches the heights of its sublime destiny only when, matching with its own genius the genius of composition, it imbues the musical work with a voice worthy of it, becoming like the revelation of divine thought.'

If we tone down the terminology as well as the 'period' purple, this is a very modern analysis of Liszt's interpretative genius.

In Defence of the Piano
A fragment of a letter to Adolphe Pictet, published in the *Gazette Musicale* (11 February, 1838).

'You too were surprised to see me so exclusively occupied with piano works and so slow to enter the field of symphonic and dramatic composition. You could not have guessed-you touched on a sore spot. You do not know that to speak to me of abandoning the piano is to speak of a sad day for me. A day that would shine over all the early part of my life and be inseparably bound up with it. For you see, my piano is to me what his ship is to the sailor or his steed to the Arab, even more perhaps, for until now my piano has been myself, my voice, my life. It is the most secret repository of everything that excited my mind during the fiery days of my youth; in it are stored all my desires, all my dreams, all my joy and all my pain. Its chords quivered under my every passion, its soft touch obeyed my every whim, and yet you, my friend, would like me to abandon it, to chase after the greater renown of dramatic or orchestral success? Oh, no! Even admitting everything you no doubt admit too freely, that I am already ripe for harmonies of that sort, my steadfast desire is to put aside piano study and development only when I have done all that can possibly be done, or at least everything I am capable of doing now.

Perhaps this sort of mysterious feeling which makes me so attached to the piano is an illusion, but it is still very important to me. In my eyes the piano is at the head of the hierarchy of musical instruments; it is the most widely cultivated, the most popular of all. It owes this importance and popularity in part to the harmonic power it alone possesses. And as a result of this power it has the faculty of concentrating and summing up within it an entire art; it spans the whole orchestral range in its seven octaves, and one man's ten fingers are enough to render the harmonies produced by the collaboration of more than a hundred concerted instruments. Works become known through its medium that might remain unknown or known only to a few people owing to the difficulty of getting an orchestra together. Thus it is what engraving is to painting; it multiplies it, conveys it, and even though it does not render its colouring, at least it renders its light and shade.

By the progress already made and through the untiring efforts of pianists, the piano is extending its assimilatory powers more and more every day. We play arpeggios like harps, drawn-out notes like wind instruments, 'staccato' and a thousand other passages which formerly seemed the special attribute of such and such an instrument. Future developments in the manufacture of pianos will undoubtedly give us the range of sounds we still lack. Pianos with a bass pedal, polyplectrums, clavier-harps and several other, as yet incomplete, attempts are witness to the generally felt need for extending it. The organ with its expressive keyboard will naturally lead to the creation of pianos with two or three keyboards and these will complete its uncontested supremacy. Nevertheless, while still lacking this essential condition, namely diversity of sound, we have been able to obtain satisfactory symphonic sounds that our predecessors had no conception of. The arrangements which have been made of the great vocal and instrumental works indicate by their poverty and their unrelieved vacuity what little confidence people had in the instrument's resources. Timid accompaniments, badly arranged songs, truncated passages and thin chords betrayed rather than conveyed Beethoven's or Mozart's thought. Unless I am deceiving myself, I was the first, in the piano score of the *Symphonie fantastique,* to give an idea of another way of doing

131

things. As if I were translating a sacred text, I paid particular attention not only to transcribing scrupulously the musical structure of the work to the piano, but also to its detailed effects and the multitude of harmonic and rhythmic combinations . . . . Henceforth, no one will be permitted to *arrange* the works of the masters as shabbily as was done at the time . . . . Once these arrangements, or more properly speaking these disarrangements, are no longer acceptable, this name should by rights only fall on the infinite number of caprices and fantasies we are swamped with, which only consist in plundering themes of every conceivable kind and tacking them together any old how . . . .

On the one hand, therefore, the piano has this power of assimilation, this universal life concentrated in it, and on the other hand it has its own life, its growth and individual evolution. To use a classic expression, it is both microcosm and microtheism, a little world and a little god. Considered from the point of view of individual progress, the number and value of the compositions written for it assure it an incontrovertibly preeminent place. Historical research would reveal not only an uninterrupted succession of famous performers since it was invented, but even of transcendent composers who interested themselves in this instrument rather than any other . . . . ' (Here Liszt develops a rather lengthy argument on Mozart, Beethoven and Weber.) 'Then, look here, I must confess I am still close to the days when I was made to learn lines of La Fontaine by heart, and in the back of my mind I always have the story of the greedy dog who let the juicy bone he was carrying go, to chase reflections in the water and was nearly drowned. So let me gnaw my bone in peace; the day may come only too soon when I will drown chasing some enormous, elusive shadow.'

A Heedful colleague
An excerpt from a letter written by
Liszt to Camille Saint-Saëns.

'My Honoured Friend,

Your kind letter promised me several compositions of yours I was expecting . . . and while waiting for them I would like to thank you again for sending me your second concerto, on which I warmly congratulate you. Its form is very new and well found; the interest in the three pieces increases and you have kept in mind the pianistic effects without sacrificing any of the composer's ideas – an essential rule in this sort of work.

First, the Prelude on the G minor pedal note is striking and commands attention. After such a happy find, you were wise enough to reproduce it at the end of the section, this time accompanying it with several chords. Among those things I particularly liked and noted were: the chromatic progression (the last line of the Prelude) and the one which alternates between the piano and the orchestra (starting with the last bar on page 5, later repeated for piano alone on page 15). The pattern of thirds and sixths in demisemi-quavers gives a charming sound (pages 8 and 9) and it merges superbly into the fortissimo entry; the zestful rhythm of the second movement and the 'allegro scherzando' on page 25; the latter might have benefited from a more elaborate development, either of the principal or some subsidiary theme; for instance the following harmless counterpoint would not seem out of place to me:

The same for pages 50 to 54 where the simple straightforwardness of the phrasing and the sustained chords of the accompaniment leave a slight vacuum. I would like to see some episodic, some polyphonic involvement here, as the Germans of this school call it; however, please forgive me observing these details, M. Saint-Saëns, I have only risked doing so while assuring you in all sincerity that I find your work as a whole singularly pleasing . . . . '

Poor Thalberg

Extract from a letter to Marie d'Agoult, February 1837.

'I have just heard Thalberg. Really, this is a complete mystery. Of all the things I know that are called superior, it must surely be the most mediocre. His last piece (a recent composition) on "God Save the King" is even well below mediocrity. I remarked to Chopin:

"He is a failure as an aristocrat and even more of a failure as an artist . . . ." '

Poor Thalberg (encore)

Part of an article by Liszt in the *Gazette Musicale*, July 1837, an article that was part of a series. *The Letters of a Bachelor of Music.* The first two of these were dedicated to 'M. George Sand'.

'Up to now I have refrained from mentioning a musical dispute that has been the object of a great deal too much attention, since it obtrudes itself on you even in your solitude and, as even you have asked me for an explanation of something which was originally the simplest thing in

135

the world but has become, as a result of comment, quite incomprehensible to the public and by means of misinterpretation has become a painful and irritating subject to me; I mean what some have been pleased to call my rivalry with M. Thalberg.

You know that when I left Geneva at the beginning of last winter, I did not know M. Thalberg; even the echoes of his renown had only faintly reached as far as us . . . . On my arrival in Paris the musical world talked of him as a pianist unquestionably the like of which no one had ever heard before, who was going to regenerate art and who, both as a performer and composer, had opened up new paths we must all attempt to follow.

You, who have seen me endlessly listening to each and every rumour, eager and enthusiastic for any progress, can imagine how my heart was thrilled by the hope of a great, powerful impetus being given to the entire present generation of pianists. Only one thing put me on my guard. That was the promptness with which the disciples of the new Messiah forgot or rejected everything that had gone before.

I felt less optimistic, I must admit, about M. Thalberg's compositions on hearing them praised to the skies in such an autocratic way by people who appeared to be saying that everything which had gone before him – Hummel, Moscheles, Kalkbrenner, Bertini and Chopin – was relegated to oblivion by the mere fact of his coming. Finally, I was impatient to see and to know for myself these new and profound works which were to reveal a man of genius to me. I conscientiously stayed indoors one whole morning in order to study them. The result of these studies was quite the opposite to what I had expected. Only one thing surprised me and that was the general effect produced by such hollow, mediocre work. I concluded that the performing talent of their author must be stupendous, and having formed this opinion, I expressed it in the *Gazette Musicale* without any malicious intentions other than doing what I had often done before; speaking my mind either favourably or unfavourably on piano works I had taken the trouble to examine. I certainly did not intend here more than elsewhere, to chide, or to dictate to public opinion. Far be it from me to claim such an impertinent right. But I thought I might, without any objection, say that if this was the new school, I did not belong to

136

it. And that if this was the road M. Thalberg was taking, then I had no aspirations to follow in his footsteps; and finally that I did not think there was in his thoughts the germ of an idea for the future which others ought to cultivate. What I said, I said reluctantly, compelled, so to speak, by the public who had made a point of placing us side by side, depicting us as running in the same arena and contending for the same laurels; perhaps it was also an innate need for men so constituted as myself to react against injustice and to protest, even on the slightest pretext, against error and bad faith, which drove me to put pen to paper. Having expressed my sincere opinion to the public, I told the author himself the same thing when we met later. It gave me pleasure to do him full justice on his talent as a performer and he seemed to understand better than others that my conduct had been candid and fair. It was then announced we were *reconciled,* and variations on this new theme were played at length and quite as stupidly as they had been on that of our *hostility.* In fact, there was neither hostility, nor reconciliation. Because one man does not grant another artistic merit that the masses seem exaggeratedly to have accorded him, are they necessarily enemies? Are they reconciled because apart from artistic questions, they mutually appreciate and esteem one another?'

Steam Concert
Caricature by Granville

LISZT AND THE ORCHESTRA

Besides Liszt's considerable contribution to the piano, an area in which he revealed himself as the creator of modern technique, it is also worth examining his achievements in the field of symphonic music. He loved this equally.

It is often said that Liszt invented programme music and the symphonic poem. This is not quite true, or at least it should be qualified, since it is not that simple.

The term 'programme music' denotes an aesthetic. The term 'symphonic poem' denotes a type of music. The symphonic poem belongs to programme music; one might almost say that in the beginning was programme music.

Now this, far from being invented by Liszt, had existed for some time. Without going back to the Greeks or the Pythian Nome evoking Apollo's battle with the dragon, in recorded times we can find programme music by Jannequin, Froberger, by Kuhnau especially, by Vivaldi in *The Four Seasons,* by J.S. Bach in the *Capriccio on the Departure of a Beloved Brother*, etc. There are many more examples.

It is rather difficult to define, in view of the many factors that enter into its composition, but the best and most complete account of the nature of programme music is D.M. Calvocoressi's precise definition:

'True programme music is either imitative, descriptive or representative, and its structure and the order of the succession of its themes, developments and colours are influenced by considerations which are not exclusively musical but which are related at least in part to the order of succession of the themes, the development and colour of the poetic subject or the story that has been chosen as a programme. Thus one can conceive of programme music which is strictly concrete even down to the faithful imitation of sounds, and programme music which is a mainly abstract and symbolic evocation of ideas or, midway between these, simply impressionistic programme music.'

All the different varieties of the symphonic poem can be considered as a poem for orchestra, the word poem being taken in its modern sense, since the basis of the work is a poetic outline. But we should also not forget its etymology, the Greek verb *poiein* which means 'to make'.

If the symphonic poem existed — or rather, had begun to flicker into life — long before Liszt, in more or less developed forms, whether vocal or instrumental, he not only brought it to its highest peak of perfection, but he also drew up its theory. Having said this, we should not forget that in this he only followed and perfected what was suggested to him by Berlioz's works.

Writing in 1837, Liszt set out its general theoretical principles, which tally exactly with what he later achieved on a musical level. This essay places Liszt's symphonic poems in the category of psychological, but in no way descriptive, even less imitative, programme music.

'The programme has no other aim but to allude in advance to the psychological motives which led the composer to create his work and which he attempted to incarnate in it .... He may have created it under the influence of specific impressions, of which he wishes to make the audience fully and wholly conscious.'

While on this subject, we should also bear in mind what he wrote in the same vein in explanation as to why and how he had composed the *Années de pèlerinage* (see page 30).

If Liszt refused to imprison himself in description, it is nonetheless worth remarking that some of his symphonic poems contain certain descriptive elements and that he endowed his own conception of programme music with a whole gamut of extremely subtle and varied shades of meaning according to the subject with which he dealt. Thus, in *Hunnenschlacht* where he was inspired by a purely visual element, a painting, we are very close to description. The horse ride in *Mazeppa* and the ball in *Tasso* move a little further away from it but there still remain clear traces. He moves even further from it towards the purely psychological in *Prometheus* and *Hamlet,* where what is evoked are no longer events but characters. In *Heroïde funèbre* and *Hungaria* we are moving even more towards the general, the abstract (besides, here we are dealing with evocations concerning collective subjects, not individuals). Finally, with *Les Préludes, Die Ideale, Ce qu'on entend sur la montagne, Orpheus* and *Festklänge* we have arrived at symbolism, meditation and the philosophically or morally abstract.

In this collection of works which, properly speaking, constitute the symphonic poems, it is advisable to include two other extremely important works, the 'Dante' Symphony and the 'Faust' Symphony. Although these two are written in symphonic form, they nonetheless stem directly from the same spirit, the first being rather descriptive or picturesque, while the other is essentially psychological.

I should like to dwell at a little more length on the 'Faust' Symphony as it is one of the most sublime and perfect of Liszt's achievements in the orchestral field. But beforehand, I would like to examine his symphonic music briefly, not so much from the aesthetic viewpoint, as from that of its sound.

Liszt's contribution in the field of orchestration is no less original than in other fields previously considered. One can certainly find traces of Berlioz's and Wagner's influence on him. But such exchanges are natural on the part of these three great innovators who were contemporaries of one another, who were exposed to the same atmosphere and the same ideas. Despite these influences, Liszt is very individualistic and daring in his orchestration and as Gabriel Pierné very rightly pointed out, he may stand as a precursor in this respect too.

Liszt's instrumentation is often very rich and full, as is much Romantic instrumentation, but contrary to that of Germans like Schumann or Brahms, it is never thick in texture. On the contrary, despite its richness, its search for power and brilliance and its accumulation of effects, it has an ethereal quality. Liszt's orchestral work always remains very incisive even in moments of the greatest stress. In this, he anticipates Richard Strauss, an orchestral virtuoso who was his disciple in many respects, and even Gustav Mahler.

One could also say that Liszt, being the virtuoso he was, is often very demanding of his instrumentalists. He exploits the technical and sound potential of the orchestral instruments almost to their limits, even to the point of using them as soloists which, for the orchestras of the time, was very daring.

Among the techniques he used habitually, one can include the doubling which, besides being so typical of Wagner's music, gives his music its special inner volume; and also his rather excessive habit of piling on the string section in wholesale unison with the wind section, a formula that Wagner again turned to good use.

But he also knew better than anyone else how to divide the quartet extremely subtly into neat portions, thus allowing full scope for his indefatigable rhythmic invention.

As the colouring of his symphonic poems required particularly powerful and varied sound resources, he drew appreciably larger resources than were commonly in use at the time. Often the orchestra had a quadruple wind section with an enlarged percussion section and sometimes special instruments or effects (for example, the tam-tam in *Ce qu'on entend sur la montagne*, a tam-tam which conducts a curious dialogue with a solo violin at the peak of a display of virtuosity; with the strings attacked with the wood of the bow — 'col legno' which only Berlioz had used before him).

Liszt was one of the first to give an important role to the harp, and to adopt the harp 'glissandi' which impressionist music abused later, sometimes so sickeningly. He also frequently used the classical instruments in unusual registers, in such a way as to obtain altogether new sound effects (for example in the 'Mephistopheles' movement of the 'Faust' Symphony.

Finally, in instrumental notation itself, he discovered methods of phrasing that generated new effects. He refused to accept the traditional forms which govern the treatment of each instrument according to its nature, and preferred to apply forms usually used for other instruments. Thus he frequently entrusts to the strings patterns whose configuration essentially belongs to the piano.

The preceding are some of the main characteristics of Liszt's orchestral artistry.

In the following brief analysis of the 'Faust' Symphony, we will see how he puts all this into practice, and we will have the opportunity of seeing in this symphonic triptych how he also puts into practice the cyclical concept we have already seen him use in his sonata.

The 'Faust' Symphony

If Berlioz's *Symphonie fantastique* revealed the potential of programme music to Liszt, it was Berlioz who, in 1827, similarly introduced Liszt to Goethe's *Faust* which he did not know at the time and of which Gérard de Nerval's translation had just been published in France. Nor should it be forgotten that Berlioz was later to dedicate to Liszt his *Damnation of Faust,* which includes that astounding Hungarian March whose sole reasons for existence are its vertiginous instrumental achievement on the one hand and the tribute of the French to the Magyar maestro on the other.

The subject of Faust, which also attracted other Romantic composers (Schumann, Wagner and Spohr, to name only the more serious ones, not to mention the project Beethoven had in mind at the end of his life), had at first naturally inspired Liszt to write an opera. To begin with, he had thought of collaborating with Dumas or Nerval, but in the end (although he later added a finale with chorus and a tenor solo composed on the concluding *Chorus mysticus* of Goethe's *Faust,* Part 2) the symphonic, thematic and instrumental impetus of the work he had in mind was enough and he contented himself with this symphony which is a symphony only in basic essentials and is more accurately a triptych of symphonic poems. The original title is *Eine*

143

Faust-Symphonie in drei Charakterbildern, (that is to say, in three psychological portraits). This clearly means he did not intend to produce a symphonic picture parallel to the plot but only to give an essential synthesis of the three main characters. This conformed with the intentions he had stated in his manifesto on programme music. And although Liszt did not formally specify this it did not displease him to let people think the two male parts (Faust and Mephistopheles) could be taken as representing two aspects of his own personality, while the central section (Gretchen) was symbolic of his idea of women. As with the *Années de pèlerinage,* the initial pretext is seen through the mirror of Liszt's own personality which submits Goethe's dramatic poem to a psychological and lyrical synthesis.

In the first section, 'Faust', the exposition opens lento with a mysterious chromatic theme, symbolising Faust's metaphysical unease:

(Incidentally, it should be noted that this is an almost perfect dodecaphonic series and that Wagner used the same pattern for Sieglinde's sleep in Act II of *Die Walküre:*

Next comes the second motif stated by the oboe, a very characteristic one with its descending seventh, which recurs frequently throughout the whole work. This is the love theme:

These two themes are later combined and developed in the slow introduction, leading to an 'allegro agitato ed appassionato assai', opening with the third tumultuous theme in the strings, followed by the whole orchestra:

A fourth heroic, triumphal theme then appears characterising the man (brass):

All this thematico-psychological material is later used with great dramatic dynamism throughout the piece which has none of the usual shape of the symphonic Allegro. In accordance with the free principles of the symphonic poem, it follows the flights of the composer's invention with a feeling for skilfully arranged contrasts between the meaning and sound effects, even going so far as to superimpose these different elements. The brilliant coda naturally makes use of the fourth (heroic) theme and comes to its climax and the second (love) theme with the 'cellos and double-basses.

The sweetness and tenderness of the second section, 'Gretchen', is in natural contrast to the preceding *Sturm und Drang*. The flute speaks out prettily, gracefully and simply above a slender harmony. Then the oboe, accompanied by the viola, presents Gretchen, the character:

In this introduction it can be seen how Liszt uses the instruments as soloists. Moreover, the only picturesque, descriptive intent in the work is the girl plucking the daisy; 'He loves me, he loves me not':

The Faust themes are then interfused with Gretchen's theme, either in reverie or in passion. Here again, there is a completely free symphonic development, without any preconceived plan, and a wonderful use of the quartet. This piece passes through all the nuances

146

of courtship, a lover's dialogue; the last bars ending on a discreet return to Faust's heroic theme, symbolic of the latter's triumph.

The third section, 'Mephistopheles', is peculiar in that it has no theme of its own. Liszt explained this by saying that Mephistopheles was the spirit of denial (*'Ich bin der Geist der stets verneint'*), and that he assigned certain of Faust's themes to him, deforming and caricaturing them — a further sparkling example of his ability with variations and cyclical forms. Faced with such thematic complexity, we can only cite a few examples here of the way in which Liszt 'Mephistophelises' certain Faust motifs. Here is what becomes of two of the main motifs, first the initial theme, his metaphysical unease:

then the theme of his heroic virility:

This whole movement has the character of a Satanic dance, in turn weird, with its truly stormy instrumentation, or sarcastic and burlesque in its patterns and rhythms. Only the Gretchen theme, heard just once in the middle of the piece, escapes Mephistopheles' diabolical intrusion and occurs with all its simple purity in the course of the grinning, infernal dance. But the dance suddenly stops. The devil disappears. The Gretchen theme, now expanded, returns on French horns and 'cellos, backed up by a new aspect of the heroic Faust theme.

LISZT AND SACRED MUSIC

It is difficult to define Liszt's position as a religious composer, because of his often baffling attitude to religion itself. Nevertheless it deserves examination in the light of certain characteristic examples, for the catalogue of Liszt's works includes a large number of what are often notable scores that were inspired by his faith. Nor should it be forgotten that the greater part of these religious works have been inexplicably neglected and that musicologists, performers and choir-masters have the task of resurrecting the substance of these treasures. Although Liszt's faith was unwavering, its manifestations were not always exalted. We know that between his youth, when his Catholicism blazed romantically under Lamennais' influence, and his maturity, when under Princess Wittgenstein's moralistic guidance despite occasional bouts of impatience, he developed it, there was quite a long period when he was not at all preoccupied by this sort of thing.

One ought also to note that most of these religious works were written before Liszt took orders, the more important works being composed during the Weimar period. Equally, it should be observed

149

conducting St. Elisabeth.

that his religious inspiration manifested itself not only in pure liturgical music, or in oratorios, but also in a number of piano compositions starting with the *Harmonies poétiques et religieuses* (the first outlines of which stem from his period of romantic Catholicism during the 1830s) up to the two *Légendes* and the last book of the *Années de pèlerinage* composed when he was middle-aged. So Liszt's career and output in this field do not always follow a logical pattern. However, is this not further proof of the 'rhapsodic' manner of the life he led . . . .

He was always conscious of the attraction religious music held for him and in this context it is worth quoting this passage from a letter to Princess Sayn-Wittgenstein dated Vienna, 16 September 1856:

'I have taken a serious stand as a religious, Catholic composer. Now this is an unlimited artistic field and I feel I have a vocation to cultivate it vigorously. I am writing another Mass to be played at Kalosca next year, where the Archbishop is having considerable repairs and restoration done on the church, which will be completed by next summer, and in '58 I will write a third for some similar occasion. The intelligent fraction of the clergy immediately adopted me after the first performance of the 'Gran' Mass and the number of my enthusiastic supporters among ecclesiastics is ever increasing. The fact is, and I think I can say this in all good faith and without pretention, that among the composers I know, none has a more intense and deeper feeling for religious music than your humble servant. Furthermore, my earlier and renewed studies of Palestrina, Lassus, Bach and Beethoven, who represent the summit of Catholic art, have contributed a great deal and I am fully confident that in three or four years I will be in full possession of the spiritual field of religious music which has been taken up by dozens of only mediocre men for the last twenty years, who, to tell the truth, will not miss the opportunity to reproach me with not writing religious music. This would be true if their trumpery counted as such. Here, as elsewhere, it is a matter of 'going back to the foundations', in Lacordaire's phrase, and reaching those living sources which continue to spring up even in eternal life.'

The last lines of this letter are of special interest in the way in which on the one hand they stigmatise an extremely regrettable state in the history of Western religious music and on the other hand define Liszt's tendencies in the matter. In fact, it is certain that the rebirth of religious music during the latter part of the nineteenth century was largely due to these ideas of Liszt's who, in order to 'go back to the foundations' and 'reach those living sources', found his inspiration in plainsong as well as in certain venerable popular airs. His unearthing of the richness of Gregorian music and its integration into modern religious music were of capital importance for the later evolution of this music. And however rudimentary Liszt's technique may have been, the benefits are still being felt, even today.

Having said this, the Lisztian concept of sacred music still remains very romantic, however great his desire to purify and hallow the genre. Not only do his oratorios indisputably take on the tone of the musical theatre (and this is not entirely contrary to its origins) but the mould of his masses and psalms are often closer to operatic arias and remind us that Liszt was one of the masters of the symphonic poem.

Some of his sacred works are even of a markedly subjective nature. It should be remembered that he composed his XIIIth Psalm, 'weeping blood' as he wrote to Brendel, at a time when he despaired of ever seeing his marriage to the Princess take place. And in the words of the XIIIth Psalm 'How long wilt thou forget me, O Lord? How long shall I take counsel in my soul, having sorrow in my heart daily? How long shall mine enemy be exalted over me? Consider and hear me, O Lord, my God . . . I will sing unto the Lord, because he hath dealt bountifully with me.' Besides, in this same XIIIth Psalm, David's complaint is given to a tenor whose lyricism is more theatrical than the tone one normally gives to prayer. It is easy to answer this by saying there were precedents for it without going back as far as Monteverdi or Bach and that musicians such as Haydn or Mozart had not acted otherwise. Sometimes, certain pieces in Haydn or Mozart masses resemble the finales in baroque opera. Therefore it should not surprise us that Liszt's 'Gran' Mass is not entirely free from some of the forms prevalent in the opera of his day.

Rather than citing purely liturgical works here as typical examples of Liszt's religious compositions, let us examine two oratorios in fairly

The Legend of St. Elisabeth by Moritz von Schwind, frescoes at the Wartburg in Eisenach.

different styles to which he endowed a very special, original quality: *St. Elisabeth,* a theatrical oratorio, and the *Christus,* a religious oratorio.

Liszt was partly inspired to write *St. Elisabeth* by the frescoes at the Wartburg in which Moritz von Schwind depicts the main episodes in the miraculous life of Saint Elizabeth of Hungary. The composer used a libretto by Otto Roquette.

The first part is in three episodes. The first opens with an instrumental prelude based on the two main themes evoking the two facets of the central character, Saint Elisabeth. First of all, her sweetness, her charity and sanctity:

Following the Lisztian technique we alluded to earlier, this theme is borrowed from a liturgical one. It is an adaptation of the hymn *Quasi stella matutina.* Then another theme evokes Saint Elisabeth's aristocratic and Hungarian origins, a theme which is both noble and popular:

These two basic themes are often repeated during the work, both in the cyclical manner used by Liszt in his symphonic poems and in that of the leitmotif systematically used by Wagner in his operas.

After an instrumental prelude, the first scene, which takes place at the Wartburg, stages the presentation of the young Elisabeth, a

Moritz von Schwind, see p.152.

Hungarian princess, at the court of the Landgrave Hermann, whose son, Ludwig, she is to marry. The girl is greeted with joyous songs, children's choirs and words of welcome. This already has a very theatrical mood, although the proportions Liszt gives to the symphonic and vocal development do not lend themselves to proper stage action.

The second scene is devoted to the 'Miracle of the Roses'. Following a custom (which displeases Ludwig), Elisabeth goes among the poor and distributes alms, hiding the bread in a flap of her gown. She suddenly sees Ludwig returning from the hunt. He draws near her and begins to reproach her, asking her to show him what she is holding; trembling, Elisabeth opens the flap; the bread has been transformed into roses. Here again, Liszt employs a style of musical dialogue that derives more from the theatrical than the oratorio. On the other hand, after the 'Miracle of the Roses', the choirs comment on and praise the event in a style which is not at all theatrical. Besides, it is on a Gregorian pattern:

In the third scene we see Ludwig leaving for the Crusades. In the 'Miracle of the Roses' he thought he had understood that God had ordained him to go and fight for the Holy Places. This martial and almost exclusively choral scene belongs to a concert oratorio style. Liszt's religious intentions are plain since the Crusaders' march uses the Gregorian theme we heard earlier, in another guise:

while the choral theme, 'Liebster Herr Jesu', provides a central expressive episode to this march:

154

The second part also has three scenes. The first is essentially theatrical. It is probably the most wholly dramatic episode in the work, where Liszt's lyrical declamation comes closest to the Wagnerian technique. We learn that Ludwig has died in the Crusades. Countess Sophie, his mother, an ambitious, wicked woman, seizes power. After conversing with her steward, she has Elisabeth appear before her, then drives her from the Wartburg as a violent storm breaks. The scene is correspondingly violent, full of dramatic dynamism where the very themes assume dramatic form, derived as much from Countess Sophie's character as from the situation. For example:

Following on the latter and contrasting with it, the second scene opens with the end of the storm during which Elisabeth fled. Abandoned and exhausted, the young Princess feels she is about to die. She considers her past life for a moment, then turns to God completely, thanking him, recommending her soul to him, entrusting her children to his care while the poor she helped or saved from want surround her and soon close her eyes. Here again, in an episode which tends towards peace and introspection, Liszt is halfway between theatre and oratorio. But he is far from realist theatre and on the contrary allows symbolic and supernatural factors to intervene.

The third scene of the work develops this symbolist, supernatural allegory. After a short symphonic episode of a nobly mourning nature, fleetingly cut across by typical motifs from the preceding themes, we come to the glorification of Elisabeth. The crowd of poor and the soldiers surround the Hungarian and German bishops in the midst of whom the Emperor Frederick pays the Church's supreme homage to the saint.

Right through this dramatic legend, from whose lines we can only draw attention to the most typical here, Liszt makes a visible effort to

155

quench his ardent romanticism. But even though he succeeds, despite himself, this attitude of mind still leaves an operatic stamp. Besides, this contrast is what lends the work such originality and special emphasis, showing us one of the most significant aspects of Liszt's religious musical inspiration.

His *Christus,* in complete contrast, is very different in inspiration. If *St. Elisabeth* is an opera which tends towards an oratorio, the *Christus* is an oratorio in which only a few dramatic strains can be heard in the distance. Completed five years after the preceding work (although both were in hand simultaneously at one period), the *Christus* reveals a very definite evolution in Liszt's thought and technique. The most significant thing here is the fact that the composer first decided to take a poem by Ruckert as his text: but this solution appeared too profane, and he wrote his own Latin libretto composed of extracts from the

Moritz von Schwind, see p.152.

Holy Scriptures and more especially from the narratives and prayers liturgically linked with those feasts that celebrated the episodes in Christ's life he wanted to evoke; Christmas, the Epiphany, the Passion and Resurrection, a triptych which conditions the outward form of the work.

No doubt the subject in this case tended less towards theatre than to church or concert hall. This is not only noticeable in the general characteristics of Liszt's score, but also in the technical treatment he used. Thus on the one hand there are a far greater number of Gregorian motifs than in *St. Elisabeth,* but these motifs are no longer used as themes serving as a basis for the development of symphonic structure. They are used just as they are, both for their typical liturgical significance (in some measure as ecclesiastical leitmotifs), as also for the lovely form of their simplicity and archaism. And so we can see how profound was the evolution of Liszt's religious thought in musical terms.

In this instance he followed in some measure the example of the oratorios and passions of J.S. Bach, in the same way as he followed it in the general arrangement of the *Christus;* in the German master's 'Christmas' Oratorio, each part is also dedicated to a liturgical feast.

Contrary to the inspired showmanship of *St. Elisabeth,* the *Christus* is as it were stripped of all means of expression, in all dimensions. Here we no longer have the gipsy speaking, only the Franciscan. Having said this, we must not think we are faced with an abstract work; moderate romanticism still plays a part in it and, as we shall see, evangelical poetry and vividness are there as well (just as they are in Bach's passions and oratorios). But all this is viewed from the angle of suggestion, inner meditation, self-effacement, and it is doubtless because of this deep humility on the part of a great orchestral virtuoso, that this work has often been misunderstood.

Starting with the prelude, the evangelistic poetry appears in the first motif of the first part, 'Christmas'; it is Gregorian in character and pastoral in expression:

There follows the evocation of Bethlehem with another pastoral theme, stated on the oboe:

Then an angel sings of the coming of the Lord, returning to the Gregorian theme:

A chorus 'a cappella', of a completely liturgical nature, no longer descriptive, sings the 'Stabat Mater speciosa'. Then Liszt returns to the evangelical and pastoral with the Adoration of the Magi, who come in to the air of an ancient hymn:

which rises little by little into a triumphal song:

After this comes the march of the Kings, where Liszt uses a Gregorian pattern, treated with the greatest harmonic simplicity; but it is also very modern and is not without a slightly exotic air:

This first section is the most developed part of the work.

The ensemble of the second part, 'After the Epiphany' is strictly liturgical in musical appearance, particularly as to the first episode ('The Beatitudes') and the second *('Pater Noster')* which is textual:

(Liszt also adapted this *'Pater Noster'* for piano.) This whole opening is typical of Catholic ritual psalmody. In the third episode ('The Foundation of the Church'), the tone changes and verges on a concert mood in the way in which the orchestra and chorus are employed. The fourth ('The Miracle') has the orchestra evoke Jesus calming the storm in a freely descriptive manner. The last episode ('The Entry into Jerusalem') has the same tendency as the preceding one but also brings in the chorus.

The third part, 'Passion and Resurrection', first comprises an instrumental prelude on sorrowful strains where one of the more dramatic intentions of the work becomes apparent. The first sung episode, *'Tristis est anima mea',* sustained on the same expressive tone, is rather in Monteverdi's spirit of pathos. It is also the only passage of this kind we find in this work, relinquishing as it does the serenity of the ensemble, attaining an almost baroque, Italianate style. This marks a much stronger contrast with the following episode, *'Stabat Mater dolorosa',* reverting as it does to the traditional motif of the liturgy:

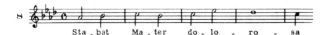

This motif is stated by the mezzo-soprano and answered by the chorus. The episode is developed in a very lovely atmosphere of sacred feeling. We should note one of the ways in which Liszt takes advantage of the Gregorian line, hardly modifying it and harmonising it just as subtly:

The following episode textually brings in the traditional Halleluja and *O filii* motifs. Finally, we have the only piece which is at all classical in nature and style; the *Resurrexit,* a fugue whose subject is taken from the *Christus vincit.*

The transfiguration of Liszt, in the style of Raphael (caricature by Borsszem Jankó)

Liszt waiting for his pupils, Weimar 1884

LISZT AND MUSIC
The *Gazette Musicale,* 16 July 1837.

One more day and I will be leaving. Free at last from a thousand ties more imaginary than real, those with which man so childishly allows his willpower to be shackled, I am leaving for the unknown lands my hopes and longings have long inhabited.

Like a bird breaking the bars of its restricting prison, fancy shakes out its stiff feathers and takes wing. Happy the traveller, happy a hundred times over! Happy the man who never does the same thing twice, who never follows the same track twice. Happy, in short, he who knows how to break things off before being broken by them!

It specially suits an artist to pitch his tent for an hour and not to build a solid home. Is he not always a stranger among men? Is his native land not elsewhere? Whatever he may do or wherever he may go, he feels himself an expatriate. It seems to him he has known bluer skies, a warmer sun, kinder souls. What can he do to assuage his vague sadness and indefinable regrets? He must sing and go on through the crowd, tossing his thoughts without worrying where they will fall, without listening to the clamour stifling him, without looking to see what ridiculous laurels are placed on his head. An artist's fate is sad but great! It is sealed at birth. He does not choose his vocation, rather his vocation takes hold of him and leads him on. Whatever adverse circumstances, opposition from the family, or society, the dark grip of poverty, apparently insurmountable obstacles, his will is still firm and invariably remains pointing towards his goal. For him, the goal is art, the sensitive reproduction of what is mysteriously divine in man and creation. The artist lives alone . . . .

Today the artist lives outside the social community. For the poetic factor, that is mankind's religious factor, has disappeared from modern governments. What could they have to do with an artist or poet, they who think the problem of human happiness can be solved by extending certain privileges and by the unlimited growth of industry and selfish comfort? What do they matter, these men who, *useless* as they are to the governmental machinery, travel through the world kindling the sacred flame of noble feelings and sublime rapture, their works satisfying the indefinite need for beauty and greatness that exists, more or less stifled, deep-down in most hearts? The fine days no longer exist when art spread its floral branches over the whole of Greece, intoxicated by its scent . . . the sublime did not surprise anyone and great works were as frequent as the great deeds which both produced and inspired them. The powerful, austere art of the Middle Ages which built the cathedrals and called to the bewitched populations on the notes of the organ, flickered and died with the faith that had imbued it. Today the bond of sympathy which unified art and society, giving the one its power and brilliance and the other those thrills which give birth to great things, is broken.

Social art no longer exists, yet has not begun. And what do we most commonly see today? Sculptors? No, manufacturers of sculpture. Painters? No, manufacturers of painting. Musicians? No, manufacturers of music. In short, a great many *artisans* but no *artists*. This is just another cross to bear for the man who has the native pride and independent spirit of a real child of the arts. He sees about him the rabble of these manufacturers, eagerly attending to the whims of the vulgar herd, assiduously humouring the fancies of the unintelligent rich, obeying their every sign. So quick to doff their caps and bow down that they seem never to feel close enough to the ground! He must accept them as brothers and see the crowd confuse them with him in the same vulgar appreciation, the same childish, vacuous admiration. Let no one tell me this is injured pride or self-respect. No, no, you know this only too well, you who are so high no rivalry can ever affect you. [This article in the *Gazette Musicale* was dedicated to 'M. George Sand'.] The bitter tears which sometimes fall from our eyes are those of the worshippers of the true God who sees his temple filled with false idols and the stupid masses kneeling before these stone and clay gods, abandoning for them the altar of the Madonna and the cult of a living God . . . .

You may find me very morose today . . . . But I have just lived through six months of petty struggle and almost stillborn efforts. I have deliberately exposed my artistic soul to all the offences of social life; day by day and hour by hour I have suffered the torments of this continual *misunderstanding* between an artist and his public which it seems must exist for a long time yet.

The musician is incontrovertibly the worst off of all in this sort of relationship. Hidden away in his study or studio, a poet, painter or sculptor carries out the task he has set himself and finds a bookseller to distribute him, or museums to exhibit him. There are no intermediaries between him and his judges. Whereas the composer is of necessity obliged to have recourse to incapable or indifferent interpreters who often make him undergo the ordeal of a translation, often a literal translation, it is true, but one which only imperfectly renders the author's thoughts and genius. Or else if the musician performs himself, for those rare occasions when he is understood, how many times must he abase his deepest emotions to a cold, mocking audience, throwing off his soul, as it were, in order to snatch a little applause from the inattentive crowd! Even so it is with great difficulty that the fires of his enthusiasm cause a glimmer on those glacial brows or light a spark in those hearts void of love and feeling.

I have often been told I have less right than others to complain thus, since from childhood my *success* greatly exceeded my talent and aims. But it was precisely because of this applause that I became convinced this was just an inexplicable vagary of *fashion* and that most of this success was due to the authority of a great name and a certain verve in

164

performance rather than to a feeling for truth and beauty. There are thousands of examples. As a child, I often amused myself by playing a schoolboy prank, which never failed with the audience. I would play the same piece, either saying it was by Beethoven, or Czerny or was my own. The days when I passed it off as my own, my success came in encouragement and patronage; 'Not at all bad for his age!' they would say. On days when I played it as Czerny's nobody listened. But when I played it as being by Beethoven, I never failed to ensure encores from the whole audience . . . .

If is a fact today that very few possess any degree of musical education . . . . Most people are content to hear, from time to time, and quite without discrimination, a few fine works and a host of pitiful things which distort their taste and accustom the ear to the shabbiest commonplaces. As against the poet, who speaks a universal language, and who besides speaks to men whose minds have been more or less formed by compulsory study of the classics, the musician speaks a

Liszt with his pupils.

mysterious language which, in order to be understood, needs special application or at least a long acquaintance. He is also at this disadvantage with painters and sculptors inasmuch as the latter appeal to a feeling for forms which is far more general than that deep understanding of the nature and feeling for the infinity which are the very essence of music. Can there be any improvement in this state of affairs? I believe so, and I also believe that we are tending towards this from all sides. One hears endlessly that we are living in an age of transition; this must be truer of music than anything else. It is undeniably sad to live in these times of barren labour when those who reap do not sow or those who harvest do not enjoy, where those who conceive salutary thoughts cannot see them come to life and, just like a woman who dies in childbirth, bequeathes them still naked and weak to the generation that will trample on her grave. But for those who have faith, what do the long days of waiting matter?

Key chart, manuscript page by

Ms. 175

Catalogue of Works

N.B. This extended chronological catalogue of Liszt's work is drawn mainly from Peter Raabe's work, and from the 1954 edition of *Grove's Dictionary of Music and Musicians*. Given the number of pages a complete list would have required, we have not given full details of the works falling within the following three categories: *works based on folk themes; songs and lieder; arrangements and transcriptions.* In these three categories only a few particularly characteristic works are mentioned.

Opera
1824-25   Don Sanche ou le château d'amour

Sacred Choral Works

1840	Five choruses with French texts (Racine, Chateaubriand, Liszt)
1845	Hymne de l'enfant a son réveil
1846	Ave Maria I
	Pater Noster II
1848-69	Missa quattuor vocum ad aequales concinente organo
1853	Domine salvum fac regem
	Te Deum — Hymnus SS. Ambrosii et Augustini
1855	'Gran' Mass (Graner Messe)
	Psalm XIII
1855-67	Christus — Oratorio
1855-59	The Beatitudes
1857	The Legend of St. Elisabeth
1858	Festgesang zur Eröffnung der zehnten allgemeinen deutschen Lehrerversammlung
1859	Psalm XXIII
	Psalm CXXXVII
1860	Psalm XVIII
	An den heiligen Franziskus von Paula

Pater noster I (gregorian)
Responses and antiphons
1862   Cantico del sol di San Francesco d'Assisi
1863   Christus ist geboren I — Weihnachtslied
        'Slavenio Slavno Slaveni!' for the millenary of SS. Cyril and
        Methodius
1865   Missa choralis
        Ave maris stella
        'Crux!' — hymne des marins
1867   Dall'alma Roma
1867   Hungarian Coronation Mass
1867-71 Requiem
1868   Mihi autem adhaerere
1869   Psalm CXVI
        Ave Maria II
        Inno a Maria Vergine
        O salutaris hostia I
        Pater noster III

	Tantum ergo
1871	Ave verum corpus
	Libera me
1874	The Legend of St. Cecilia — Oratorio
	Die Glocken des Strassburger Münsters
	Anima Christi sanctifica me
	St. Christopher
1875	Festgesang zur Enthüllung des Carl-August-Denkmals in Weimar (Der Herr bewahrt . . .)
1876	'O heilige Nacht' — Weihnachtsgesang
1878	Septem sacramenta
1878-83	12 Chorales
1878-79	Via Crucis
1879	Cantantibus organis — Antifonia per la festa di Santa Cecilia
	O Roma nobilis
	Ossa arida
	Rosario
1880	Pro Papa
1881	Psalm CXXIX
1883	Zur Trauung
	Nun danket alle Gott
1884	Quasi cedrus (Mariengarten)
	Qui seminant in lacrimis
1885	Pax vobiscum
	Qui Mariam absolvisti
	Salve regina

Secular Choral Works

1841	Four 4-part male choruses (for the benefit of the Mozart-Stiftung)
	Das deutsche Vaterland
1842	'Wanderers Nachtlied' (Goethe)
	Das düstre Meer
1842-47	Titan
1842-57	Für Männergesang — collection of 12 male choruses
1843	Trinkspruch
1844-51	Les quatre élémens
1845	Festkantate zur Enthüllung des Beethoven-Denkmals in Bonn
	'Le Forgeron' (Lamennais)
1846	'Die lustige Legion' (Buchheim)
1848	Arbeiterchor
	Ungaria-Kantate
1849	'Licht, mehr Licht'
	Chorus of Angels from Goethe's Faust
1850	Chöre zu Herders entfesseltem Prometheus

	Festchor zur Enthüllung des Herder-Denkmals in Weimar
1853	An die Künstler
1857	'Weimars Volkslied' (P. Cornelius)
1859	Morgenlied
	Mit klingendem Spiel
1869	Gaudeamus igitur
1870	Kantate zur Sekulärfeier Beethovens
1871	Das Lied der Begeisterung
1875	'Carl-August weilt mit uns': Festgesang zur Enthüllung des Carl-August-Denkmals in Weimar
1883	Ungarisches Königslied — 6 choruses
1885	Gruss
	'Es war einmal ein König' (Goethe)

Orchestral Works

1860	Two Episodes from Lenau's 'Faust'
1860-66	Trois odes funèbres (Lamennais, Michelangelo, Tasso)
1863	Salve Polonia
1865	Rakoczy March
1867	Ungarischer Marsch zur Krönungsfeier
1875	Ungarischer Sturmmarsch
1880-81	Second Mephisto Waltz
1881-82	From the Cradle to the Grave

Works for Piano and Orchestra

1830   Malédiction — with string orchestra

1834   Grande Fantaisie Symphonique, on themes from Berlioz's 'Lélio'

1849-61   Concerto No.2 in A major

1848-52   Fantasia on themes from Beethoven's 'Ruins of Athens'

1849-56   Concerto No.1 in E flat major

1849-59   Totentanz

1851   Schubert's 'Wanderer Fantasia'
           Weber's 'Polonaise brillante' Op. 72

1852   Fantasia on Hungarian folk tunes

Chamber Music Works

1832-35	Duo Sonata for violin and piano (based on a mazurka by Chopin)
1837	Grand Duo Concertant sur la romance 'Le Marin', for piano and violin
1874	Elegy in memory of Countess Maria Moukhanoff, for 'cello, piano, harp and harmonium
1877	Elegy No.2 for piano, violin and 'cello
1880	Romance Oubliée, for piano and viola or violin or 'cello
1881	Die Wiege, for 4 violins
1882	La Lugubre Gondola, for piano and violin or 'cello
1883	Am Grabe Richard Wagners, for string quartet and harp

Works for Piano

1. ÉTUDES

1822	Variation on a Diabelli Waltz
1824	Huit Variations
	Sept Variations brillantes sur un thème de G. Rossini
	Impromptu brillant sur des thèmes de Rossini et Spontini
	Allegro di bravura
	Rondo di bravura
1826	Études en quarante-huit exercises dans tous les tons majeurs et mineurs (only 12 were written)
	Scherzo in G minor
1838	24 Grandes Études (only 12 were written)
1838-51	Études d'execution transcendante d'après Paganini
1840	Mazeppa
	Morceau de salon — étude de perfectionnement
1848	3 Études de concert
1851	12 Études d'exécution transcendante
1852	Ab Irato — Étude de perfectionnement de la 'Méthode des méthodes'

| 1862 | 2 Concert Studies |
| 1868-80 | Technical Studies — 12 books |

2. ORIGINAL WORKS FOR PIANO

1834-52	Harmonies poétiques et religieuses
1834	Apparitions — 3 pieces
1835-36	Album d'un Voyageur — 3 books, 19 pieces
1835-55	Années de pèlerinage, 1st year, Switzerland: 1. Chapelle de Guillaume Tell. 2. Au lac de Wallenstadt. 3. Pastorale. 4. Au bord d'une source. 5. Orage. 6. Vallée d'Obermann. 7. Eglogue. 8. Le mal du pays. 9. Les cloches de Genève.
1836	Fantaisie romantique sur deux mélodies suisses
1838-49	Années de pèlerinage, 2nd year, Italy: 1. Sposalizio. 2. Il Penseroso. 3. Canzonetta del Salvator Rosa. 4. Sonetto 47 del Petrarca. 5. Sonetto 104 del Petrarca. 6. Sonetto 123 del Petrarca. 7. Après une lecture de Dante, Fantasia quasi Sonata (Dante Sonata)
1839	Tre sonetti del Petrarca — 1st version
1840-59	Venezia e Napoli — supplement to the 'Années de pèlerinage': 1. Gondoliera. 2. Canzone. 3. Tarantella
1841	Albumblatt in E major
	Feuilles d'album in A flat major
1842	Albumblatt in waltz form
	Elégie sur des motifs du prince Louis-Ferdinand de Prusse (nephew of Frederick the Great)
1845-48	Ballade No.1 in D flat major
1848	Romance
1849	Grosses Konzertsolo — for the piano competition of the Paris Conservatoire
1849-50	Consolations — 6 pieces
1851	Scherzo and March
1853	Ballade No.2 in B minor
	Sonata
1854	Berceuse
1859	Prelude after J.S. Bach

179

1862	Variations on 'Weinen, Klagen, Sorgen, Zagen'
1863-65	Deux Légendes: 1. Saint François d'Assise. La prédication aux oiseaux. 2. Saint Francois de Paule marchant sur les flots.
1864	Urbi et orbi – bénédiction papale
	Vexilla regis prodeunt
1865-76	Four short pieces
1868	La Marquise de Blocqueville – Portrait en musique
1870	Mosonyis Grabgeleit
1872	Impromptu
1872-77	Années de pèlerinage, 3rd part, Italy: 1. Angelus! Prière aux anges gardiens. 2. Aux cyprès de la villa d'Este – Andante 3/4. 3. Aux cyprès de la villa d'Este, Threnodie II – Andante non troppo lento. 4. Les jeux d'eau á la villa d'Este. 5. 'Sunt lacrymae rerum', en mode hongrois. 6. Marche funèbre. 7. Sursum corda
1874-76	Weihnachtsbaum – 12 pieces
1874-77	3 Elegies
1877	Sancta Dorothea
1880	In festo transfigurationis Domini nostri Jesu Christi
1881	Wiegenlied (chant du berceau)
	Nuages gris
1882	La lugubre gondola
1883	R.W. – Venezia – after Wagner's death
	Am Grabe Richard Wagners
	Nocturne d'après un poème de Toni Raab
1885	Recueillement
	Historische ungarische Bildnisse
	Trauervorspiel und Trauermarsch
	En rêve, nocturne
	Unstern, Sinistre, Disastro

3. DANCES

1836-50	Grande valse di bravura
1838	Grand galop chromatique
1840	Galop de bal

1841	Galop in A minor
1842	Petite valse favorite
1843	Ländler in A flat
1849	Festmarsch zur Säcularfeier von Goethe's Geburtstag
1850	Valse impromptu
	Mazurka brillante
1851	2 Polonaises
1856	Preludio pomposo
1881-82	Csárdás macabre
1881-83	3 valses oubliées
1883	Mephisto polka
1884	2 Csárdás

4. WORKS BASED ON FOLK THEMES

The abundance of works in this section makes it impossible to give details here of each of the hundred or so pieces it comprises; they draw on the folk music of Czechoslovakia, England, France, Germany, Italy, Poland, Russia, Spain and Hungary. But it is worth reserving a special mention for the 19 *Hungarian Rhapsodies,* whose composition dates extend from 1846 to 1885.

5. WORKS FOR TWO PIANOS

1834	Grosses Konzertstück über Mendelssohns Lieder ohne Worte
1856	Concert pathétique

6. WORKS FOR PIANO DUET

1861	Notturno in F sharp major
1876	Festpolonaise, for the marriage of Princess Marie of Saxony
1880	Variations on 'Chopsticks'

Songs and Lieder

The 80 songs and Lieder Liszt has left us cannot be listed here — songs which set texts in all languages, and range from Béranger to Goethe via all the literary trends of the period.

Recitations with Piano Accompaniment

1858	Lenore (Bürger)
1859	Vor hundert Jahren (Halm)
1860	Der Traurige Mönch (Lenau)
1874	Des toten Dichters Liebe (Jókai)
1875	Der blinde Sänger (Tolstoy)

Works for Organ

1850	Fantasia and Fugue on the Chorale 'Ad nos salutarem'
1855	Prelude and Fugue on the name Bach
1860-84	2 Vortragsstücke
1863	Pio IX, der Papsthymnus
1864	Ora pro nobis, litanie
1877	Resignazione
1879	Missa pro organum lectarum celebrationi missarum adjumento inserviens Gebet
1883	Requiem für die Orgel
	Am Grabe Richard Wagners

Arrangements and Transcriptions

As is generally known, arrangements and transcriptions, whether for piano or for orchestra, constitute a quantitatively important part of Liszt's output. The complete list of them comprises about 350 items, among which we find the most disparate composers, from Bach and Allegri to Verdi and Saint-Säens; naturally they also include transcriptions which Liszt himself made of his own works. However, mention may be made of some of the most characteristic arrangements:

1835   Réminiscences de 'La Juive' (Halévy)
1835-36   Réminiscences de 'Lucia di Lammermoor' (Donizetti)
          La Serenata et l'Orgia. Grande Fantaisie sur des motifs des 'Soirées musicales' (Rossini)
1836   Grande Fantaisie sur des thémes de l'opéra 'Les Huguenots' (Meyerbeer)
1838   'Soirées italiennes'. Six amusements pour piano sur des motifs de Mercadante
          Schubert Lieder
1838-39   Schubert's 'Schwanengesang'
1839   Beethoven's 'Adelaide' (Op.46)

1840	Mendelssohn Lieder (Op. 19, 34, 47)
	Fantaisie sur des motifs favoris de l'opéra 'La Sonnambula' (Bellini)
1841	Réminiscences de 'Norma' (Bellini)
	Réminiscences de 'Robert le diable' (Meyerbeer)
	Réminiscences de 'Don Juan' (Mozart)
1846	Tarantelle di bravura, d'après la Tarantelle de la 'Muette de Portici' (Auber)
1848	Wagner's Tannhäuser Overture
1849	Beethoven's 'An die ferne Geliebte', song-cycle Op.98
	Extracts from Wagner's Tannhäuser
1852	'Soirées de Vienne'. Valses caprices, d'aprés Schubert
1859	Concert paraphrase on Verdi's 'Rigoletto'
1860	Extracts from Wagner's 'Flying Dutchman'
	Six chants polonais, Op.74 (Chopin)
1861	Valse de l'opéra 'Faust' (Gounod)
1867	'Tristan and Isolde': 'Liebestod' (Wagner)
1872	Lieder by Robert and Clara Schumann
1882	Réminiscences de 'Boccanegra' (Verdi)

N.B. To this catalogue, which already totals 686 items, one should properly add 15 unfinished works, certain of which are very important, e.g. *Sardanapale,* an opera in three acts based on Byron, and *St. Stanislaus,* an oratorio on a text by Princess Sayn-Wittgenstein.

Moreover, one should also mention 166 doubtful or lost works, which are nevertheless expressly mentioned in the Liszt biographies.

Lastly, no mention has been made of the countless publications by musicians of all kinds which Liszt revised.

Literary Works

Most of Liszt's important writings were collected in the seven volumes of the *Gesammelte Schriften*, edited by Lina Ramann and published by Breitkopf and Härtel. Many of these works were undoubtedly written by the composer himself but we may also be sure some of them were drafted by Marie d'Agoult or Princess Sayn-Wittgenstein.

The following are the names of the studies that are of particular interest today:

On the religious music of the future 1834
On the position of the artist and his status in society 1835
Letters from a Bachelor of Music 1835-1840
Robert Schumann's piano works 1837
F. Chopin 1852
Gluck's 'Orpheus' 1854
Beethoven's 'Fidelio' 1854
Weber's 'Euryanthe' 1854
Beethoven's music for Egmont 1854
Mendelssohn's music for 'A Midsummer Night's Dream' 1854
Richard Wagner ('Tannhauser', 'The Flying Dutchman',
     'The Rheingold') 1849-1855
Berlioz' Harold Symphony 1855
Robert Schumann 1855
Clara Schumann 1855
John Field and his Nocturnes 1859
The Gipsies and their Music in Hungary 1859
A critique of the critics: Oulibichev and Serov 1858

LISZT SOCIETY

A Liszt Society was founded in London in 1950:

Secretary	—	Humphrey Searle
Address	—	44A Ordnance Hill, London, N.W.8.

ADAM
ANNA

MARIE DE FL/

BLANDINE LISZT*
1835-1863
ép. EMILE OLLIVIER en 1857

ép. HA

DANIEL OLLIVIER
1863-1941
ép. CATHERINE DU BOUCHAGE

DANIELA SENTA VON BULOW   BLANDIN
1860-1940
ép. Dr. THODE

BLANDINE OLLIVIER
ép. PREVAUX

DANIELA DE PREVAUX   CLAUDE DE PREVAUX
ép. JEANSON

BLANDINE
CISIMA
AIRANE
MARIE-SOPHIE

French line

Liszt's three children by Marie d'Agoult, née Flavigny, were called Flavi

ADAM
ANNA

SSE D'AGOULT

DANIEL LISZT*
1839-1859

en 1857   ép. RICHARD WAGNER en 1870

ON BULOW   ISOLDE WAGNER   EVA MARIA WAGNER   SIEGFRIED WAGNER
                  1865-1919   2867-1943   1869-1930
A   ép. Dr. BEIDLER   ép. HOUSTON STUART   ép. W. WILLIAMS

              FRANZ BEIDLER   WIELAND
                                                                 FRIEDLINDE
                                                                 WOLFGANG
                                                                 VERENA

German line

legitimized by the Empress of Austria and were then called Liszt.

189

190

Selected Bibliography

ORIGINAL SOURCES

Franz Liszts Briefe, ed. La Mara. 8 vols. Leipzig, 1893-4.

Franz Liszts Briefe an Baron Anton Augusz, ed. Wilhelm von Csapo. Budapest, 1911.

Franz Liszts Briefe an seine Mutter, ed. La Mara. Leipzig, 1918.

Franz Liszts Briefe an Carl Gille, ed. Adolf Stern. Leipzig, 1903.

Briefe hervorragender Zeitgenossen an Franz Liszt, ed. La Mara. Leipzig, 1895, 1904.

Briefwechsel zwischen Franz Liszt und Hans von Bülow, ed. La Mara. Leipzig, 1898.

Briefwechsel zwischen Franz Liszt und Carl Alexander, Herzog von Sachsen, ed. La Mara. Leipzig, 1909.

Briefwechsel zwischen Wagner und Liszt. Leipzig, 1919.

Correspondence de Liszt et de Madame d'Agoult. Paris, 1933. 2 vols.

Comtesse d'Agoult. Mémoires. Paris, 1927.

WORKS IN ENGLISH

Liszt's Letters, ed. Constance Bache. London 1894.

Letters of Liszt and von Bülow, ed. Constance Bache. London, 1898.

Correspondence of Wagner and Liszt, ed. Francis Hueffer. London, 1888.

Letters of Franz Liszt to Marie zu Sayn-Wittgenstein, ed. Howard E. Hugo. Harvard, 1953.

Lina Ramann. Franz Liszt as Man and Artist. 1 vol. only translated. London, 1882.

James Huneker. Liszt. London, 1911.

A. Habets. Letters of Liszt and Borodin, ed. Rosa Newmarch. London, 1895.

Amy Fay. Music Study in Germany. London, 1893. Re-published, New York, 1965.

Janka Wohl. François Liszt. London, 1887.

Life and Letters of Sir Charles Hallé. London, 1896.

Constance Bache. Brother Musicians. London, 1901.

Guy de Pourtalés. Franz Liszt, the Man of Love. London, 1927.

William Wallace. Liszt, Wagner and the Princess. London, 1927.

Sacheverell Sitwell. Liszt. London, 1934; revised edition, 1955. Re-published New York, 1966.

Ernest Newman. The Man Liszt. London, 1934. The Life of Richard Wagner. London, 1933.

Memoirs of Count Albert Apponyi. London, 1935.

Ralph Hill. Liszt. London, 1936.

Cecil Gray. Contingencies. London, 1947.

'Liszt' in Grove's Dictionary of Music, 5th edition. London, 1954.

Walter Beckett. Liszt. Master Musicians. London, 1956, revised edition 1963.

Bence Szabolcsi. The Twilight of Franz Liszt. Budapest.

New Hungarian Quarterly. Liszt-Bartók issue. Budapest, 1962.

Hunphrey Searle. The Music of Liszt. London, 1954. Re-published New York, 1966.

Illustrations

We are particularly grateful to Mademoiselle Irène Vassiliev for giving us the pictures by Moritz von Schwind on pages 152, 153 and 155.

The assembling of illustrations for this volume would not have been possible without access to the invaluable collection in Robert Bory's La Vie de Franz Liszt par l'Image (Horizons de France).

Archives Photographiques, p.185 – Archives Seuil, p.138 – Bibliothèque du Conservatoire (Ed. du Seuil), pps. 22, 116, 167 – Bibliothèque Nationale (Ed. du Seuil), pps. 29, 32, 42, 49, 50, 56, 63, 65, 67, 84, 87, 98, 101, 103, 108, 125, 127, 128, 129, 130, 132, 133, 135, 148, 168-184 – Bibliothèque de l'Opéra (Ed. du Seuil) p. 110 – Bulloz, pps. 24, 34 – Giraudon, pps. 135, 189 – Harlingue, pps. 6, 14, 18, 47, 109 – Louis Held, pps. 161, 165 –,Richard Wagner Museum, p. 94 – Centre Hongrois de l'Institut International du Théâtre, p. 41 – Roger Viollet, pps. 2, 144.